Consider the Feast

Carmit Delman

Published by Open Books

Copyright © 2019 by Carmit Delman

Interior design by Siva Ram Maganti

Cover image © Foxys Forest Manufacture shutterstock.com/g/Foxys

ISBN-13: 978-1948598231

1.

"This London leg is a beast," 20B smirked. "Please say you're either wildly funny or a drunk like me."

I clicked my backpack into the bin above and slipped past him to the window seat.

The man extending a handshake resembled an ancient marble bust—bald, thin-lipped, and haughty like Caesar. A jaunty bowtie around his neck softened him somewhat and seemed to say that he could laugh at himself. Still, I could see that he was a force, and at half an hour till takeoff, tucked into a blanket, he'd already somehow charmed himself a gin. "Philip," he offered.

Suddenly weary from my pilgrimage, I sank into the seat. "I'm Talia."

"Talia." He tasted my name carefully. "Beautiful name; beautiful woman."

I was not impressed. "You're the guy who says that to everyone."

"Not to everyone, trust me. The world's full of monsters."

And from that moment on, everything I tell you is a confession. You've asked me about The Quarter, and maybe as you say, now that almost two decades have passed, its stories should be chronicled for the sake of history. True, the place was a wonder during that time of plenty, its streets filled with countless stories, sweets and magic-makers at every turn. And of course there was Prongs. But the story I must own is the one that started on that plane ride.

By the time we were in the air en route to New York, Philip seemed like an old friend, if a dizzying, eccentric one. At nearly sixty, he was full of energy and old-world mannerisms but wholly indifferent to ordinary decorum. He had, he told me, first made his name as a builder, transforming historic churches into million-dollar condos. In his fifties, he wrote several well-known Hollywood movies, one right after the other. Thinking he was ready to slow down, he became Chair of the English department at Channing College near where I had grown up in New York. But then, a few years later—on a whim and to impress some long-gone lover—he'd decided that slowing down was for the dying, and he started producing Food Shows for network television, too.

"And you?" Philip asked me, as if I, at nearly thirty years his junior, should have such a story.

"Divorced mom. Once a playwright, now freelancing ad copy."

Fresh out of graduate school, I'd written a play that had had a short but acclaimed run off-off Broadway. The premise was a character, much like me, sitting down to dinner with four people, much like my dead grandparents. From my father's side, they took a flight together from Mumbai. From my mother's side, my grandmother came in from the quiet green cemetery where we buried her in Israel. Last to arrive was her husband, who rose up from the refugee camp where they met, married, and had my mother. That camp was where he died, in limbo—after surviving the anonymous dust and bones of Auschwitz, and only one month before the family reached the Promised Land.

In the play, it was just me and the four dead folks. We ate, we drank, and they told me their war stories. Over dessert, my maternal grandma in unthinking habit caressed the numbers tattooed on her arm, while her husband boasted that his hometown borscht recipe trumped all other borscht recipes, as if he would someday taste that borscht again, as if something small like a recipe could mean anything after a Holocaust.

Meanwhile my paternal grandma told the table in hushed tones, "It makes us sick, of course, forbidding the servants to sit on the furniture. We are educated people, you know." She jutted her chin in the direction of the girl she had brought with her from Mumbai, who was clinking and cleaning dishes in the other room. "But that's how they are—give a finger, they'll take the hand." She and Grandpa both nodded and stared wistfully Stage Right, certain and sad, because the girl would have to sleep again on the floor that night.

The play was a small work, at times clumsy. And it was less art, more a mere hiccup of some inner life. I was, after all, only one or two generations removed from these experiences of concentration camps and caste and hardship, which were imbedded in the DNA that passed to me. So they haunted me; and if fate had leaned this way instead of that, I myself could easily have been somewhere else instead of here, in need or in slavery or entrenched deep in a complicated place of knotty moral frameworks that would not seem knotty at all to me. I too might see wisdom and love firstly as my father's mom described it to me, a sour-sweet duty. So the play was in some ways merely a clannish memory I'd conjured up that happened to sound just musical enough as it emerged. But it was not without promise...

"Decently received," I told Philip, though he had never heard of the play or the director, and the theatre, he informed me, had closed the previous year. "Some critic declared it 'The Progressive's Progress,'" I shrugged. "Whatever that means."

"A good quote," he chuckled, "if you don't think about it too hard."

The Progressive's Progress. I remembered that quote in particular of all the others, because though I didn't really understand what it meant, the mention of Progress struck me as a mission, a calling. Like somehow it channeled all the general uneasiness I had with the world, which I would never have been able to name or pin down at that point, but which had something to do with the haves and the have-nots. That reviewer knew that *I* knew something was wrong out there. And the play hit upon it with some post-colonial, post-racial, post-religious, post-everything stream that was actually resonating. If the review was right, there could be more plays. And, there could be...*progress?*

"After that," I told Philip, "I thought maybe I would be like one of those babies born with teeth. You know the ones?" He looked at me blankly. "It's rare but it happens sometimes—that babies come right out gnashing these little pre-natal teeth. And those unusual people, planted somehow by the cosmos, they are known for carrying the world's history on their shoulders. Napoleon Bonaparte was born with teeth. And Julius Caesar." I cleared my throat, embarrassed to admit that I had hoped to be like them.

"After my play closed, I tried to conjure up that force and voice again. I wrote half plays, sketched out others, but couldn't manage to produce another finished work. Around the time I met Jack, it began to dawn on me that maybe I never would. So I needed to be swept up in a foreign energy, and that first night, as he and I watched each other from across the café, he eventually sat down wordlessly at my table, beaming as if he knew that I wanted him there. I did. Up close, pale and blue-eyed, he looked so familiar. Five months later we were married."

Philip nodded knowingly.

"Are you with him?" I was asked over and over by strangers glancing from me to my husband—from my colors and bearing back to his colors and bearing. "Are you together?"

"Yes, we're married." This seemed to seal something for them, and because of that, for me, too. My life had to be framed differently now that I'd allied myself with someone from Connecticut, someone freckled and uncomplicated who wore crisp button-ups every day—not just for occasions—a man who would never understand the tangles behind a play like mine, who had never even watched it in full, just fast-forwarded through an old recording of it. But the way people were mystified at our union made me feel distinct, like some cell that had separated and mutated, changing the zigzag of evolution.

Maybe it's just me, I thought, as I became absorbed into his tall-good-looking-white-man reality, where he was a confident marvel. Parking spots opened up right where we needed them and waitresses offered us things that weren't on the menu—and the universe itself seemed to defer to him. For a time, I was included in the contentment of majority, privy to the good ole boy's club, and in on the joke. So I wondered, maybe those tangles had just been my own edge all along, or only imagined? Maybe my uneasiness with the world was merely my own self-obsession, some grudge I had dreamed up and then nurtured till it came to life. So I clung to this prospect, almost hopefully, and brought it with me to a house at the edge of the city.

"And the writing?" Philip asked, adjusting his airplane blanket.

"You know those little weeklies at the grocery store?"

"With in-store coupons and cake recipes?"

"Someone's got to write them." I shrugged. "Now you know who."

"Where in Israel did your grandmother live anyway?" he asked as the flight attendant approached with her trolley. Put off by the very thought of airplane food, Philip produced from his jacket a wedge of Stilton cheese wrapped in printed parchment paper and a tiny jar of cherry preserves. "I'm just now returning from filming at an archeological dig there."

"Outside Nahariya, on a farm."

The flight attendant placed a square paper napkin on my tray. "Coffee?"

From habit, I shook my head no. No coffee; that had always been my rule. When I was a child, my father had drunk eight cups a day of Sanka. He liked it hot, but he would take it at any temperature, sand-bottomed, sweetened with saccharine and powdered creamer, even lukewarm and on the go in a chalky Styrofoam disposable cup. Sanka was decaffeinated, so it couldn't have been a physical addiction. But in his mind, that was how he marked the passage of time, in cups of Sanka.

When my mother's mother learned that she had terminal cancer, we moved to her farm in Israel for a few years to live with her while she died. My mother brought with us boxes of Sanka, and each morning in Israel my father would sit on the stoop drinking coffee as he did research. He rested a thick book on one knee and kept a spiral pad at his side, with a collection of colored pencils for notes. Every few weeks, he took the bus to a library in Haifa, lugged back the old books and brought home new ones for his thesis on folklore.

Once, knowledge was like that, a physical act, muscles carrying hardback tomes, eyes straining, a wetted finger pulling apart rice paper pages and then trailing line after line into the trillions. There was a certain stamina required to bore through a block of information, which became an ancient librarian's rite once technology allowed anyone to snappily access the breadth of any subject. Suddenly the screen was everything, a portal to anonymity, to contain some infinite frontier, and it seemed knowledge didn't need to be pursued anymore; there was an expectation that curated right-answers could be passively downloaded. And with that change there was something more fragile demanded of success—more than mere bullish memorization, or privileged access. It was some trembling inspiration or gimmick, some wisp of viral luck. But from my father's stolid presence on the stoop during those years, knowledge would always feel connected to the physical motions of the body, part of some art and learning that has been lost, even to me.

The neighbors would smile to see him at work, a quiet bespectacled Indian academic—a novelty there. They wouldn't say anything, not in front of my mother or it would rouse her old Israeli thorniness. But I was an observant child, big-eyed and braided, and I liked to fade into the background. So I heard their whispers and saw their looks. And in my head afterwards, I tried on their personalities and ideas. I made wisecracks, trying to imitate them for the audience of my family. *A regular Gandhi*, I would say, mimicking their awkward smiles, lips pulled back over the teeth into a rectangle. *Our black Einstein.*

After the funeral, we moved back to America. My mother was still in mourning as she unpacked our boxes into a Beacon rental house. "Well, Ran, at least we are set with coffee again." It was the sort of sentence she had to muster up painfully in the moment, but that could, when the sadness passed and with enough repetition, become a good punch line to the whole few years. And it did.

For me, though, my father's sheer dependence on coffee and the drink's ghastly blackness drove me into a kind of terrified abstinence from it. I went all the way through college without drinking it, and all through the long nights of work leading up to my play. It was good to be beholden to nothing, to no one. Being attached to any habits, any objects, even caffeine, meant being fettered somehow.

"That's cheap. That's just privilege," my mother informed me as we sat on the porch once when I was visiting during graduate school. "It's meaningless, you know, to swear off attachments, when you can have them at any time. To make everything black and white and simple. Anyone who's ever had nothing before knows that." But even through my whole marriage and those sleepless years after having Aiden, when he was just a baby, no coffee.

"Actually," I stopped the flight attendant just as she was about to pull the cart away. "I'll take a tea, please." I stirred in a packet of honey and sipped carefully. "So, how was the dig?" I asked Philip who had ordered another gin, and tea, too.

"Grueling. That was their deal though—these archeologists—that we had to be there in the trenches with them. So we woke up before light to breakfast and to load the van. We worked with them all day under the broiling sun with trowels and brushes, carrying buckets of dirt in between interviews. I bagged and cleaned artifacts and labeled them, that was my specialty. My knees hurt. My back hurt. And after all that, the wind could blow enough sand over the site to destroy a full day's work. Nature is such a bitch sometimes, you know? We returned to the dorms—just cots really—in the late afternoon, showered, and ate dinner, and sometimes we managed to have a beer and to film more follow-up. But mostly we just fell into bed early."

"I can't imagine *you* doing any of that."

Philip nodded, lip curling. "It surprised me, too. But it all paid off, because I got some fascinating interviews with these archeologists who are great experts on food in the ancient world. They may even win me an Emmy. Stilton?" He offered me a soft wedge of the cheese spread with preserves. I took it between two fingers. "It's from my favorite London cheese shop. I always stop there if I can, even when I'm just on layover like today. Brown and Butter. Do you know them?" When I shook my head, he leaned in confidingly. "You didn't hear it from me, but they'll be opening a workshop at The Quarter in a few months, so you can get to them there." He cleared his throat. "Anyway, what were you doing in London this trip?"

"Actually, London is just my layover, too. I'm on the way back home from India."

"India?" He looked at me in horror. "What in hell were you doing there?"

"I'd never been before." My grandparents always told my mother and father to send me for a holiday, but for one reason or another it was put off each time, always till next year. And instead they ended up coming to us for visits. They died in a car accident when I was thirteen and my father alone flew back to say goodbye. After that, every few years, my mother or father would say, we have to plan that trip, but we never did. "And when the divorce finalized, and we decided Aiden would go to sleep-away camp, I heard about this volunteer program in the slums—"

"Of course!" Philip interrupted gleefully. "You decided to travel the world, heal lepers—maybe get laid some?"

I made a face. "I really just needed to get my head together."

He nodded. "So you went searching for wisdom."

"Maybe," I hedged.

"Don't deny it, you *are* a seeker all right, a restless type. And that's good news." Philip stretched and folded his fingers behind his head. "Because the more someone like you is out brooding, searching, trying to fix unfixable problems, doing meditation or finger-painting or Hiawaska, the more amusing it is for someone like me, who won't. *I've* never had a calling to go to India; never will. It's just not in me. I'm perfectly alive exactly where I am. Also," he added, "I gave up trying to pretend I care about anywhere as remote as India or Africa years ago."

Who even talks like this? I asked silently shaking my head as if appalled, though also perfectly used to such ennui. "Anyway, it's an astounding place. I mean, you just come out of the airport and the air itself is like nothing you can imagine."

As it happened, I put a lot of stock in the meaning of air. Soon after we met, Jack fancied himself an amateur weatherman for a while. So he bought some gear—a barometer and a rain gauge—and went to a workshop on meteorology. He told me about the teacher, A. J. Bart, a real enthusiast and something of a vigilante who would drive out to meet tornadoes or cross-check news channel weather predictions with his own and then call in to correct them. A. J. explained that air molecules could hold the essence of a place and its people. If you stop to let it in, he said, you could download it, like a memory. This guy could smell rain clouds in the air, and say with utter certainty that a downpour in New England first started gathering a week ago over the Nile River. And when they looked it up on Weather Channel maps, he'd be right. Ever since I'd heard A. J. Bart's ideas, and long after Jack's infatuation with storm-chasing had passed and the gear wound up in the trash, I was a believer and looked for data in the air. "My first breath of Mumbai air was an ancient stink—smoky, heavy, bloody. Like millions of humans skinned alive, but somehow still carrying on."

"Go on." Philip nodded, at once disgusted but also eager.

How could I explain it all? I took a taxi from the terminal and it drove through a world that no matter how many newspaper articles I read, or how many stories I heard from my parents and grandparents, I'd never truly pictured. Crowded streets and markets with swarms of bodies packed so tight that they could not be real. So many people begging, skinny children with nowhere to go, people living upon each other in layers: a grand human laundry, with washer-women, their arms like machine spinners, slapping and flattening and wringing out clothes into filthy water.

"By the time I reached the hostel, I was overcome. How did this pass for ordinary life for so many people?" I opened my phone and flipped through some photos from those first days for Philip.

"Look at you, in your movie star sunglasses!"

"I didn't take them off those first days." He enlarged one of the photos, peering into the street behind me, and then scrolled through a few more. "As if they could insulate me."

When the sunglasses weren't enough, I tried to take cover in the jostling auto rickshaws and cars and trains. But it didn't help. The machines themselves seemed to have no sense of civilization as I knew it, no seat belts or speed limits or maximum capacity. And all that air, that humanity, kept pushing itself inside. I tried a few days of the volunteering, but it became too much and I quit. And one evening in the youth hostel, I finally broke.

"What did you think it would be?" my roommate asked, patting my shoulder awkwardly when I could not stop weeping. She was an Australian backpacker, half my age, randomly assigned to the bunk above mine. "One big yoga studio?"

"No." Feeling foolish, I wiped my face with the back of one hand and pressed myself to the window with the other. Just beyond the glass, skinny bodies lay limp to their fate, stretching as far as I could see. "I just didn't know."

"You poor simple thing," Philip pouted.

"Come on," I said defensively. "I'm not some small-town girl. We live in one of the craziest places on the planet, you and me. It's a hard place too, and worldly. So I know strip clubs off the highway and Wall Street czars. And homeless people, and The Quarter," I reminded him.

"Oh, yeah?" he smirked, calling me on my bravado. "You spend a lot of time in The Quarter?"

"No," I admitted. "But the farmers' market is there. So I pass by all the time. I see some of it. I've seen that Pie guy," I added defensively. "And those hippies."

Philip made some sound of amused satisfaction, but I ignored him and returned to telling him about India. Over time, hunched under my backpack and lonely amidst millions, the initial shock of India wore off a little. People, it seems, can become accustomed to anything. And one day, I came upon a truck of men paving roads. The mile of air around them was toxic from the tar cooking and smoking. I was aghast to be downwind of them for even five minutes, covering my face against the fumes, and unreasonably angry that I should be exposed to them at all. And for the sake of those workers, part of me was horrified by the realization that the smoke, day after day, must be taking years off their lives.

Still, I saw their ordinary talking and laughing together, and I also understood that they had jobs and regular pay and went to sleep each night feeling content that they could provide for their families, so they were more fortunate than many, and unless I had something better to offer, who was I to say otherwise? And somehow with that, I acquired a shaky if passing balance in it all, so I could finally stand up and breathe and actually look around India a bit for the first time.

"Funny you ask if I went looking for wisdom," I said to Philip. "I suppose it did become some kind of hunt for a wise man." It made sense there. On any corner in India are shrines and altars, or monks doing what monks in monasteries have done for centuries: sitting on the floor, etching and pinching colored sand into an intricate mandala mosaic several feet long. Day after day they do this, stopping only for prayers and to drink tea with yak butter. And then, when the impossible mosaic of brilliant swirled sand is complete, they blow it away into nothingness to remember what we try to forget, that that is what we are, after all, nothing.

"I realized that if I looked around in this land, I could probably find some scrap of purity that would give me what I needed to go home. Some sense of purpose. And I knew that all I needed was a glimpse of it, because that moment of enlightenment would carry a lifetime. Like finding even the tiniest evidence of intelligent life on another planet would forever change our construct of the universe."

He looked at me knowingly. "You must believe in God, yes?"

"Jewish by birth," I said, unwilling to commit to more.

"*I* don't believe, of course." Philip was leaning forward intently, listening for the story, but for something more, too, something beneath it all. "But I'm always curious what it's like to be someone who does believe."

The airplane bounced up and down for a moment or two, jostling the trays of everyone aboard—hundreds of miles above the earth, at the mercy of wind and clunky machinery—asking all that very same question: Do you believe in God? For a split second, everyone on board was a believer.

Then the plane leveled, everyone doubted again, and I collected myself to continue my story.

The small town of Pushkar is set around a holy lake. It was formed, the local guide said, by the tears of Lord Shiva mourning the death of his wife. One of my first days there, I hiked up a hill to a little temple overlooking the lake. I sat and watched. Wisps of life drifted from the bleached white buildings that encircled the watery calm. Pilgrims at the Ghats immersed themselves in the water. Chanting rose like steam off the lake. From such a distance, people and beads of sunlight were nearly indistinguishable. It started to dawn on me that, probably, true philosophy and art were only ever created by people who had had the chance to sit for a time, near but not too near civilization.

I sat and watched the scene for hours, the quiet movements below, in this place that had healed people long before I was born and would be healing people long after I was dead. And when I finally hiked back down the hill, the lake pulled me to it, as if there was a physical magnetism in the quiet lapping water.

The mists rose off the lake as I neared it. And suddenly, a chanting figure emerged from the gray. It was a Hindu holy man, skinny and nearly naked but for a loincloth, and smeared in ash and red. His body seemed to be just a stringy vessel, some lean transportation, for the greater reality that was his soul.

I took a step toward the sadhu. He caught my eye and stepped toward me, too. It did not surprise me. Somehow I had almost been expecting that he would recognize me, as if he had been waiting many lifetimes only for me to seek him out. My body froze in anticipation as he neared.

"Your wise man..." Philip breathed.

"Yes."

I felt his hand on my shoulder. I held up my own hand in greeting. He broke into a wide, blithe, nearly toothless smile. We could not communicate with words, only gestures and nods.

"But if you've ever looked into the eyes of someone who has lived their entire life on the shores of a holy lake, set apart from ordinary civilization," I tried to explain, "then you will know that purity and wisdom really do exist. Maybe even God."

Philip held up his hands in defeat. "See, I'm such a cynic. I would have assumed that he was just trying to get you alone somewhere."

I sank a bit into my seat. "Well."

"Well what?" Philip straightened. "He *did* make a move on you, didn't he?"

"Not really."

The sadhu had signaled with his hands for me to come with him. I followed him around the winding ghats of the lake. Suddenly, he touched my face and hair. He put an arm around me, and held me to his frame.

"It was abrupt," I told Philip. "And it *did* seem odd. I did wonder whether he was just a frisky old man? And if I had been you, or maybe if I had been another version of me, in that moment, I would have missed it." But then I took in the breathtaking view he had wanted me to see, of the lake and the valley. From an airplane window, did it resemble Shiva's teardrop? Did it disappear altogether? "And I realized that I was the one who was off, who was broken, polluted with suspicion, and I held his hand then and we sat by the water together. It *was* unspoken and mysterious, and wise." I turned triumphantly to Philip who was wrapping up the remains of his Stilton. "So you see, it does exist. And I found it."

"Did you?' Philip tisked, unconvinced. He was quiet for a moment and then continued thoughtfully. "Let me tell you something. You know who was on our dig? Roger Cart. You've probably seen him on the History channel. He's got bright blue eyes and a ruddy goatee. And he looks exactly as Hollywood always wants an archeologist to look, so they're always putting him on these specials. Anyway, one day after the dig we drank a beer and chatted for a while. 'Why are you in archeology anyway?' I asked.

"'What kind of question is that?'

"'Let's be honest,' I told him. 'You're beautiful enough to make it on television full time. And this is tough work.'

"'I leave the heavy lifting to the students,' he winked. 'But you're right. This is about sifting through thousands of tons of dirt for a mere fragment of something that once meant *something* to *someone somewhere.* That slip of meaning is what I hunt for.'

"Roger," Philip explained, "had done his fieldwork and dissertation on the foods preserved at some ancient site in the mountains—remnants of honey, salted meats, and olive oil. 'And the things you learn about how people lived in the past, tell us everything we aren't able to learn about who we are now.'"

"So what had he learned?" I asked Philip.

Philip pressed the button on his armrest and tilted back his chair, closing his eyes for a moment. "Underneath a very thin layer, he told me, we're all just fossils of ancient empires." I felt a chill, as if Philip could see straight through me and into all the echoes of weakness inside.

"Roger told me he was writing an article about wine connoisseurs from the Bronze Age, based on some site down south where they found room after room of wine jugs with elaborate remnants of juniper and honey and cedar oil and cinnamon in thousands of extravagant combinations. 'Do you understand the importance in this?' Roger asked." Philip turned to face me. "In a single dirty room you could see the entire story of humans: The kings and players who feasted and drank and brought humanity into civilization. And the slaves they harnessed so they could." He paused and tilted his head toward me. "We tell ourselves we're a complicated spectrum of characters, but really we are all either kings or slaves."

Philip closed his eyes and drifted off to sleep. I watched him breathe for a while, the rise and fall of his chest and cheeks, slack now without his quips and sarcasm. Crazy old man, I decided. What does he know?

I pulled the blanket out from the pocket in the back of the chair before me and tucked it over legs. I shut off the light overhead. Still, I could not fall asleep. I tried to conjure up my holy man again, who had sat beside me in Pushkar, who had caressed my face and held my hand. What was his wisdom?

Strangely, I couldn't picture his face and doubted him again. I started to sweat, replaying each moment of my Indian odyssey in my head, and feeling more and more humiliated.

Of course it was a move after all. The way he had beckoned me to follow him into the maze of buildings, and when I shook my head no, the way he shrugged and motioned instead in a practiced way at my camera, for me to take a photo of us together, and then to pay him, as many tourists likely did. But why should it surprise me that a sadhu could be this base? Now and then there were movements of wakening and enlightenment and rage against the way men behaved with women. But wasn't that just the truth of human history, as much a part of our genetic food chain as tribalism and the hunt: great men, small men, even the wisest men, led by the thing in their pants?

As Philip snored softly, I heard Roger's words again, so confident in their own truth, echoing all I suspected deep down inside myself too: Kings and slaves, slaves and kings.

I closed my eyes and understood that I hadn't tapped into some wisdom at all, not in India, not anywhere. And that sadhu had been just as much without answers as me or anyone else.

———————

"So for all your hunting, you didn't find a wise man," Philip said to me, stretching as we both awakened. The cabin stirred as lights turned up and people waited in a tight line to use the lavatory. Stewardesses moved through the aisle serving drinks before preparing for landing. "But," he offered, "you did find me. And that should be worth something."

"How so?"

"Here's a proposal: why don't you come teach in my department?"

"You're offering me a job?"

"That's more than the monk had for you." He made an official appraisal. "Have you ever taught before?"

"Not really. I was a TA in graduate school," I shrugged. "And years ago, my father had mono, so on and off I finished his classes for him. But that's all. Anyway, what would I teach?"

"You're a writer. There are a few sections of Writing still open—Composition, Creative Writing, whatever's left. You'd take those." He cocked his head. "Look, you'd be doing me a favor. I'm handing off the Chair position once the semester starts, but meanwhile I have to staff these classes."

"I don't know." I hedged for some unknown reason—for being shackled to a full semester, or to this unnerving man.

"The company—meaning me—is decent, if a bit mad. And no promises, but I can probably get you your own office." He smiled smugly, like one who had never been told no. "Think about it."

"Okay," I conceded. "I will."

2.

The airport taxi let me out in front of my house, into the soft green smell of night in my yard. I breathed in deeply, at once checking the air for any change or intrusion and also just smothering myself in the goodness of home. I touched the tree bark by the path, feeling knowingly for each knot: the cluster of three that formed a face, and then the one big knot at the center. I breathed in that scent of yard, a smell I'd known for years, a particular fragrant mix of cut grass, pollen, metallic sprinkler water, and soil ribbed with clay. The smell defined this small plot of land and over time it was etched into my lungs so much so that someday, I assumed, in the last, dwindling days of my life, that smell and my child would be all that could stir me from hazy dreaming.

Above, the windows were black but then I saw a faint glow from behind Aiden's curtains. Eagerly, I let myself in, dropped my backpack by the door and hurried up to his room. I peeked inside. There was my boy, lying awake in the dark, playing on his phone. I threw myself on him.

"I didn't know Daddy was bringing you here tonight."

"He didn't." He hugged me back, tightly, but made a show of reluctance, so I should remember not to try it in public. "I took the bus." He laid the phone at his side and propped up his head with one arm to face me, smiling. The smile stopped my breath just a bit, and so did the realization: this was a boy who took the bus, who could be at home on his own. This was a boy who would soon outgrow me.

"I missed you." I pushed aside his shaggy hair. "How was camp?"

"All right," he shrugged. "The counselors were kind of useless. Great French Toast. Most of the kids weren't into Gamecraft. But a couple were." He didn't seem to have more to say about it.

I put an arm around him, taking in the near-grown up awkwardness of shiny skin and a prickly chin, but still those traces of puppy fat. His voice had started cracking lately, and each long limb seemed to have a will of its own. When he was a baby, his scent elicited that teeth-gritting adoration, which mothers often try to give fumbling shape to, smooshing bellies and cooing *I could eat you up*. Even on those nights when I lost my temper with him, just as soon as he was in bed, predictably, I berated myself, and went to tuck him in, and I'd inhale that scent as he slept. Now Aiden's aura was nearly mannish, a wave of something familiar and fleeting. When he let me hug him these days, I'd try to capture it in my lungs, too, with the scent of the yard, to hold it there—impossibly—since nothing can ever really be held.

"How was India?" Aiden asked, leaning back on the pillow with his hands folded behind his head. "Did you get it out of your system?"

"I told you, that's not why I went, wise-guy. Anyway, I'll have to show you pictures." I gulped. "I don't know if you'd believe me."

"Over breakfast?" Aiden yawned. I saw his hand reach unthinkingly for the phone glowing at his side in the dark.

When Aiden was little, Jack and I debated whether or not to get him his own technology, a tablet or pad or pocket-sized player. "Boredom is a gift," I'd declared a bit self-righteously at the time. "The screen turns kids passive—no, worse, it makes them entitled. How will they learn to create someday if all they know is how to be entertained?"

Eventually Jack bought him all the technology anyway, there was no fighting it—not Jack, not the changing of times. So the day we took Aiden to the ocean for the first time, he had already seen it through virtual reality goggles dozens of times. But when he stood on the sand in the salty wind and heard the waves erupting and saw the vastness of all of earth's black water foaming before him, it was something no virtual reality could have prepared him for. After life on-demand, with the sound and clarity tweaked to comfortable ease, the real thing was just too beautiful and spontaneous, so he yelped in fear and clung to us the whole time, hating it. I knew then we were failing him.

Any restriction on technology just made it more tantalizing when he did get his hands on it, so he had little self-control, just hunger. But in the end, had technology really made him passive, or had it somehow launched a new, strange version of living actively? Sometimes I caught glimpses of his friends, posting photos online, pouting or poised in front of luscious plates of food. They punctuated every other moment with hashtags. It was all so artfully measured and awake—more awake than I had ever been. And I wondered, did they end up experiencing more moments of their lives more deliberately than someone like me, if only for the sake of crafting those snapshots?

"Will you turn that thing off soon?" I asked Aiden, standing up and kissing his forehead. Somehow, somewhere, my directives to him had turned into mere suggestions.

"I'll think about it," he assured me as I left. Already as I closed the door behind me, he was absorbed again in the small screen.

I showered and fell into bed, exhausted. But I did not fall asleep at once. I looked over at the other pillow. Jack's pillow. Still sometimes, it felt strange that Jack was gone, hitting me like a new realization now and again. I looked up at the ceiling over my bed. I knew every inch of the ceiling, every inch of the whole house. A home was a funny place. Inside each square of walls, every family made its own little life and world, punctuating the passage of years with milestones and a sense of fierce importance. But every now and then, when I walked through the neighborhood and saw block after block of those other houses, it was clear that no single house could be that important after all.

After Aiden was born, with a child now inside it, our house became a living organ of sorts, pulsing around me, pumping and leaking, the walls vibrating from sounds or changing color and cracking over time. At first, Jack brought in some weekly help to clean the house, a Mexican woman who spoke little English. But I was never a good manager with her, always just pandering and grateful and clumsy. I couldn't comfortably delegate my toilets to a stranger when my mother had cleaned her own toilets, thank you very much. And if ever I thought of something to correct her on I would remember, mortified, how my grandparents' servant had slept on the floor, and I would say, instead, everything looked perfect.

Eventually it became clear that I wasn't going to be working outside the house anytime soon—what work would I do, and now it had to offset childcare, too. Having the help was more trouble than not, so Jack let her go. Almost in relief, I took up the toilet brush myself. And that was how I learned the house.

I started to possess intimate knowledge about tiny details of the space, the smudge on the wall that wouldn't come out, the crack in the floor, the hum the refrigerator made when its generator was slowing down. I knew where the sun entered during the evening hours, how to twist the hot water faucet back on when it was loose and useless on the pipe, and which windows would stick, which screens were torn.

There was a delicate art to living in this house and embracing those walls—or at least to feeling less restless and trapped within them. Margo Sesame catalogued that art, so in those years I devoured her home design shows and read her crafting magazines with an earnest devotion. Our home turned into a gallery of quilts, scrapbooks, and chunky knitted sweaters.

Jack, too, filled our house with the stuff that preoccupied him, knickknacks and catalogues of knickknacks. Piles of technology that became outdated after six months. Back-up pairs of glasses and sunglasses in different styles, belts in various shades of brown and various shades of tan, gimmicky kitchen appliances and bulk-bags of spices that would not be used in ten lifetimes, and materials for projects that never happened. It was almost a feat of athleticism to stay abreast of the newest products and the newest versions of the newest products, to constantly process and purchase, to compare reviews and ratings on the string of reviews that existed around every battery, model number, and product big and small. Consuming was an infinite pastime.

And indeed just as I always suspected, the more cardboard boxes of old papers and junk mail in the attic, the more gadgets, the more mixers, the more habits—the more I was anchored in one space.

Even Aiden seemed to be one of these things, too, that tied me down. I felt the weight of him, in between that sweeping awe of time and biology and the act of creation, in between the godly boasts—*I made this human*—as if we bitty beings could really have something to do with the miracle of it. When I did not watch him, I watched the plastic camera lens as it watched him, trying to catch the child in some un-childlike pose of what childhood should look like. And, we bought him more crayons and remote control cars and plastic tools and tiny tubs of play-dough, so that he, too, could start to accumulate his own material weight in the world.

With time, I began to melt into the crevices and moldings of the house. I saw myself mottled, as the way I looked in the toothpaste spattered bathroom mirror or shadowed, as reflected in the darkened foyer window, when I locked up for the night. On the days when the house was messy, I was messy too, a tattered extension of the old yellow wallpaper downstairs we never replaced. On the days when seasons changed, winter to spring, summer to fall, and new scents filled the house, I seemed full of potential, too. For a time anyway, until everything settled back into the same old creaks and patterns. And because the house was me and I was the house, I became protective over it. I dug further into the routine of freelance and carpool and volunteering for the neighborhood patrol, safeguarding this little life for as long as I could, until I couldn't anymore.

Reaching for Jack's pillow, I pulled it to me so I could spoon against it. Jack and I had slept in the same bed until the night he moved out. As soon as he was gone, it somehow freed us to be awful to each other for many months. Then one day, in the midst of the ugliest part of the divorce, as we waited outside the lawyer's office for the third time that week, I realized just how fleeting it all was. That waiting room, and that negotiation, had become our new normal. In the aquarium on the wall, I watched the blue and yellow striped fish again, same as last time, swimming in and out of the sunken ship that they had somehow claimed for themselves. And in that moment, not quite leaning against him in the chair near me, but almost touching shoulders, it felt like Jack and I again, not angry anymore, but simply resigned. "It's a terrible power."

"What is?" His eyes were tired.

"To destroy a person—this little person, *our* little person's—world."

He nodded because it was true. The only important thing here now was Aiden, and maybe it had all—the relationship, the house, all of it—just happened so that he could come along.

Had it destroyed his world? Aiden never said. Though of course, it was not like I ever asked him, and even when he seemed on his own to want to speak of our family, I shied away, frightened by what we had done. And soon our original sphere of three—familiar bodies and routines and obligations, reading books together, bored in the car on the way to the hardware store—all seemingly eternal, were suddenly gone. Certainly for Aiden, whatever life he grew into would relegate this all to the past someday. Maybe one day the pieces would even be replaced for me and for Jack—with new routines, and different people in different seats in different cars. But part of me suspected that until the end of time, nothing would ever seem real or right until this original clan said yes to it. And the pillow next to me would perhaps always seem like Jack's pillow.

———

The morning after India, I could tell from the house's echoes that Aiden was already gone for his run. I took the phone from my bedside table and scrolled through the messages. One from my parents: *Did you land safely?* Another from my parents: *Call us when you get up.* Another from an unknown number: *Did you think about it? –Philip.* I ignored the others, but at the third message from my parents, I realized there would be no avoiding it: *I'm coming by,* I texted back.

Aiden returned home to get ready for the day, but he was not interested in seeing his grandparents. "They were at camp last week visiting. Plus I have plans. Can you drop me at The Quarter?" he asked. "I'm meeting people."

I showered and dressed and slid into my car. He hopped in next to me and we drove in silence. I had been for all intents and purposes on another planet these past few weeks, but my body recognized the familiar car seat and routine at once. That same cool leather, that same old sticky wheel, the same soundless drive with him as he balled up and looked at his phone screen. Driving through my neighborhood, blinking into the sunlight, it felt like a Hollywood set after India, stark and clean and strangely unchanged, though how could it possibly still be here exactly as I'd left it, still humming obliviously?

We passed out of our neighborhood and the small commercial square at its edge and then drove the main road toward The Quarter. The street gradually went from green and spread out to a more congested, urban crowding, until we reached the top corner of The Quarter, which jutted northward and touched our street. The corner had both a bus stop and subway stop with a large train station below ground, but sometimes I just walked all the way there for the exercise.

This commercial edge of The Quarter was really all I knew. The Quarter itself extended a mile or so further downtown and was wide from side to side, having taken over large segments of several neighborhoods. I had never really entered beyond the farmers' market or seen its extent. But I had shopped at the market every week since it opened years ago, and I'd seen the posh coffee shops and restaurants while passing. So I knew the energy that buzzed around this place.

There were the eclectic eateries of course, most devoted to some micro focus: just High Tea and cucumber sandwiches and scones in one spot, another place had a wall of drawers with nothing but coffee beans from Kona and Antigua and the Ivory Coast—all over the world, so you could hand select every single bean, and mix and match if needed, until you had enough for a cup which would be carefully collected and ground and brewed into the steaming cup you desired. There were famous restaurants I had heard of, and famous restaurants I had not heard of but which people said existed behind doorways in underground labyrinths or nearly hidden between popsicle shops or mustard boutiques.

Milling around the streets, there were tourists, of course—one was wearing a Chef Yorkie t-shirt that showed him all skater-wild and covered in frosting with his catch-phrase *Let Them Eat Cake*. There were the bloggers, chronicling their market visit, uploading videos, announcing to their fans, "The cherries are in!" and posting their daily Top Ten lists. There were the recipe nerds, meticulously hunting down the exact color, ripeness, plumpness of ingredients.

There was the street performer I had mentioned to Philip, wearing just a single nude stocking over his body and part of his face and an old-fashioned curly blond wig and pearls. All day he sat silently at one corner of the farmers' market, spraying whipped cream into pie tins and eating it with a wooden kitchen spoon.

The Pie Eater received a steady clink of change in a separate pie tin, and every now and then one of the tourists put his own face close to the pie man and took a photo with him. The Pie Eater appeared not to notice and continued to fill the tins and eat the pies, gracefully and solemnly. Maybe he was accustomed to the tourists. Or maybe he was just caught up in his art.

At the far edge, there were the hippies, wearing plain linen smocks and sandals. They often slept on that corner. A pierced boy strummed a guitar and chanted quietly. A girl with flat braids passed around a wooden bowl with some heady yellow saffron tea. In the middle of the group sat a big crate of soft nectarines. Every now and then, someone would reach for a nectarine, open it with one juicy bite and then pass it around to the others, dipping the flesh into a packet of fine-cut pink salt.

"By the museum is good," Aiden suggested. I pulled in to an open parking spot right in front of the building dedicated to the history of food in The Quarter. He started to get out.

"Are your friends here yet?" I looked around.

"No. But you don't have to wait."

"I'm waiting," I insisted. He shrugged and settled back into his seat. I pointed to the museum. "I brought you here once, when you were a baby. Soon after it was built, when The Quarter expanded." It was always strange to return to places with Aiden where we had once been intertwined—me, a mother saddled with diapers and he, a dependent squashy baby, smelling of milk. Now we were just two big beings, side by side. "I think you'd fallen asleep in the stroller while I was shopping at the farmers' market, so I pushed you in here, sacks of produce tucked in around you, and I wandered for ten minutes before you woke up bawling."

Aiden only shrugged now. "Well, I'm not a baby anymore." I knew how to see through his cool demeanor. This big towering boy was still under my protection, vulnerable, looking to me for guidance, despite his large paws and feet that dwarfed mine. And yet, his compass was also shifting, it was starting to dawn on him that the real thing was out there, not in here with me. Despite all my fussing and homemaking, I was just his stopping point en route to the other place. All the millions of moments I—and Jack—had given to him, museums, changing diapers and singing lullabies and holding him up to see an animal at the zoo—were imprinted in some subconscious corner, yet long forgotten, and never truly retained by him. Meanwhile, for me, they were locked and crucial in my memory. Such an ugly and beautiful truth, that a child never knows how much a parent has given, and only knows enough to expect it.

We both watched as a big orange bus pulled up and a swarm of children belonging to a camp group filed into the museum for a field trip. All the kids wore neon green t-shirts still creased from the box that said Camp City Rise, and they were ushered inside by a few bright young men and women, who had likely once gone to Camp City Rise themselves. These adults were clean-cut church-goers, and they spoke to the campers in clipped tones, expecting to hear sir and ma'am and no funny business, because it was only with such discipline that a kid could ever hope to get out. Different but the same—they echoed the adults who had raised me, with a similar sense of rigidity, a similar mistrust that anything good could last.

"Did you ever take a school field trip here?"

"Nah. What would have been the point?"

And he was right. In the circles in which we lived, in which Aiden had grown up, which even I took for granted, there was no need to be introduced to The Quarter. Its plenty was all around us to be devoured or dismissed at will. Sometimes The Quarter came up in the news. Or there was a get-together at a particular restaurant. Tourists came in droves, of course, after visiting the Statue of Liberty or Freedom Towers. And local enthusiasts were obviously a big part of the scene, regularly there in hordes, looking for rice pudding or small-batch smoked Himalayan sea salt or handcrafted sodas in green glass retro jars, or declaring, "I'm obsessed with finding the most authentic kombucha." And all the while they laughed at their own absurdity. "First world problems, right?" If you weren't part of that and just lived nearby like me, you only came and went for shopping or business. You stopped noticing The Quarter, like it was the West Village or the Strip in Vegas where who knows what existed behind closed doors. For these campers though, all spiffy in starched green t-shirts on this big day out, what seemed so ordinary to us, was really not.

"There they are," Aiden said quickly, spotting his friends at a distance. "Bye, Mom. Thanks for the ride," he said in his old, sweet voice.

For an impossible moment, I remembered him at five, uninhibited and exuberant, rubbing his cheek against mine and wanting me next to him as he fell asleep. Then I remembered him at seven, sharper, when he could already listen to pop songs on the radio and discern the lyrics, but still he connected their over-the-top proclamations of love with loving me. Then I remembered him at ten, when I forgot to put a tooth fairy dollar under his pillow, and I scrambled to slip it in there later, not because I wanted him to believe in the tooth fairy—he already didn't—but I wanted him to still believe his mother would never forget such a thing. Then I remembered him at eleven, in the last play he'd tried out for at school, and somewhere during those months of rehearsal, he'd realized he had actually outgrown dress-up and play-acting and only went through the motions of *The Sound of Music* and when the last show was done, he put that away for good. Each smaller Aiden was swallowed by the next size up, like a heartbreaking set of Russian Dolls, until he'd become the Aiden before me now. And despite that small, rich mercy of parenting—the long stretch of tomorrow-mornings in which to start anew under the same roof—now we were closer than not to the last of it.

He opened the car door and hurried out before the others spotted him with his mother. He reached them and joined in step with their walk, and as they passed by the car, he did not look at me, but made a small wave with his hand. I recognized the other boys, some he had been friends with for years; I knew their parents. All good kids, each caught now in their own separate awkward path, pimply and sometimes gruff and hunkered into headphones but still making good grades and when it came down to it, kind.

After they passed, instead of starting to drive, I turned off the car. I got out and headed in the direction of the museum. Philip had piqued my interest again in The Quarter. It had been so long, and I was here anyway, so why not?

I passed the Pie Eater and paused for a moment to watch. A few of the campers in their green t-shirts who had straggled behind the others stood there, too. I hadn't taken the time to really watch him in years, I realized, and now that I took it all in, there was something hypnotic about his movements. He did a mesmerizing, deliberate dance, twirling a wooden spoon. His face mute under the curls and stocking, it still showed a range of emotions with darkly outlined eyebrows and lips: perplexed at one moment, furious the next, ecstatic finally tasting the whipped cream. He looked older than when I had last seen him, the wrinkles showing through his stocking. Still, all of us in the small crowd around him clapped at the end and the campers put some coins into his waiting pie tin and then hurried before me into the museum.

The museum was completely silent inside. It looked pretty much the same as it had a decade before. It was just one or two sparse galleries, and an information desk and gift shop both of which seemed to be unmanned at the moment. It was more a tourist's outpost for The Quarter than a proper museum.

One exhibit was dedicated to explaining the pervasiveness of foodie culture today, trying to finger the tipping point where it had become so mainstream and so consuming for a large part of the population. One careful placard connected it to a moment in a reality TV show, showing a continuous reel of episode 214 from *Recipe Roadtrip*, when the boisterous host discovered a two-hundred-pound hamburger at a state fair in Mississippi. Another pointed to the year in which Margo Sesame went from a chef to a full-blown celebrity and entrepreneur, with a line of pots and pans, and cosmetics. A dusty glass case held a model of the first meal delivery service box, of carefully measured, cut, and portioned ingredients, allowing people to feel that they had cooked without actually cooking and getting their hands dirty.

An exhibit in the next room talked about the history of The Quarter itself. There was a time when The Quarter was nothing but a mall in the middle of a shabby neighborhood. It had housed stores offering cheap jewelry, or jeans for teen girls, or jeans for grown women who wanted to look like teen girls. There was a food court serving lo mein and subs and soft pretzels and ice cream. And over it all was a numb halogen glow. Sesame Enterprises took it over and tore down the mall, leaving a clean outdoor plaza, and invited crafters and growers from all over the tri-state area. For a few years, the farmers' market became a thriving town center. All the homemakers like me flocked to the place with linen bags or strollers, seeking out new foods to brighten the table.

Then, slowly, the Sesames bought up neighboring streets, and during a construction rage, they transformed it all into the vast intertwined district it was now. The genius of it, one placard boasted, was The Quarter's quaint stone streets and alleys and shops of all sizes that somehow managed to evoke different materials, different eras of architecture in the facades, and different countries or cultures. Various placards talked about how the city was petitioned and the various architects commissioned, and the many countries represented there. But in truth they had all emerged at once during the savvy Sesame project.

The farmers' market was still there, but just a small part of the whole now, along with countless open eateries, peasant street food trucks, and upscale restaurants where you had to wait three years for reservations, and also the night market. It drew a whole new modish crowd.

I walked quietly through the ghostly exhibits. Here a faceless mannequin held a tray of gray shapeless impressionistic food. I leaned toward a glass case that held an open, yellowed book, an 1896 first print edition of Fannie Farmer's *Boston Cooking School Cookbook*. As I leaned back out, a gaunt man, the curator, stepped from the shadows behind, inadvertently startling me. "Do you have any questions?"

I shrieked, then calmed, and put a hand on my chest to slow the furious beating of my heart. "No, sorry. You scared me." But then I fumbled for my purse. "No one was at the front desk when I came in. How much is admission?"

"No charge." He waved this aside with a pale hand. "We are a grant-funded educational resource. Though donations are welcome."

I pressed a couple of dollar bills into his palm and was about to leave but then I turned. "Why is that?"

Folding the bills tightly between four fingers, he said, "Why what?"

"Why is this place grant-funded?"

"So people can feel like all this is theirs."

Right then the campers filed out of a back room where they had watched a short film. Some of them looked a bit bedazzled having learned of all the food that lay just beyond. With a pang of both guilt and disconnect, I realized that the curator was right: this museum was indeed for them. The many people for whom plenty and indulgence was and always would be something exotic and aspirational, even as they ate free school lunches and went to grocery stores that were deserts in their neighborhoods, soft molded cucumbers and mealy apples the only fresh things around, and nothing but candy bars for miles and miles. It was the city's way of promising, like a mother does, that you can be anything you want to be, even though she knows better.

On the road again to my parents' house, the jetlag started to hit me. Howard Stern reruns did their part, pumping circus folk and porn stars through the radio like drumbeats. But still I was fuzzy, and the drive began to slip by in yellow ribbons that unraveled hypnotically along the road. I needed a break. A quarter mile from the old Rt. 9 donut shop, it smelled like yesterday's grease. But closer it was good yeast and burnt sugar. I pulled my car into the parking lot, shaking off my drowsiness as I entered the store.

The place had the feel of most roadside shops, a grime that hovered threateningly, like the whole establishment could be boarded up at any minute. It had been that way for as long as I could remember. Over the years when I stopped here, I recognized people from high school working the counter. Eventually, they seemed from my frozen lens too old to be my peers, and looked more like their parents had. Now it was their children. Tables and chairs lined the front window, big enough to perch upon and eat, but small enough so no one would comfortably stay for too long. A dusty rack of chips sat for sale off to one side, each forgotten bag faded over time to a pale version of itself, and a small cooler of cokes, flat but icy.

Only the stocky woman behind the counter seemed alive, hair limp behind her in a low ponytail, her scrubbed ruddy face shining in defiance of the place. I had never seen her working there before, but she seemed vaguely familiar, like we had passed each other anonymously at the mall for years.

"You look like hell." The donut-lady spoke her truth to me. "You need coffee."

"I don't drink coffee," I said from habit.

"Then iced coffee," she decided.

For some reason, on this morning after India, American plenty was too hard to resist. After all the years of no, I gave in and nodded yes to the coffee. I also eyed the rows of donuts behind her, glistening, frosted slopes that draped the walls. Some were crusted in sprinkles, dusty with thick cinnamon, painted into pink and green curlicues, or punctured at the side, spilling guts of strawberry jam and cream. There were long ones, stretched into drizzled braids, and tiny ones, like glossy marbles in a pile, airy crullers, and others flattened out with dollops of sweet cheese and maple syrup. "Also, one Glazed please." I slumped at the counter, chin on one palm to watch.

"You melt the sugar first, see, using the hot coffee. Then ice. Then plenty of cream." Muscle memory moved the woman's fingers in a leathery ballet around the cup.

"There you go, honey." She capped my coffee with a flourish.

I grabbed the cup and pocketed my change on the way out. It was the extra-large size, like a vat of shortening. I placed it in the holder beside me in my car and merged back onto the highway.

I took one hesitant sip from the straw, letting the taste roll over my tongue and linger in my mouth before I swallowed it. The creamed iced concoction, and the just-a-bit-of-a-high were exactly what I needed. It quickened my blood in a gradual, then a thick, rush. I waved at truck drivers and saw the small towns passing in Technicolor hues. Suddenly, everything seemed possible as I ate my donut in soft slow bites, like flirting.

I veered off the highway toward my childhood home.

From the kitchen table, I could see all the old pictures on the fridge. There I posed, a child in sepia tones, on the farm in Israel. A photo of Jack and me under the plastic *chuppah* at our wedding was still there. Years of Aiden's school photos, starting with kindergarten, posed before a curtain backdrop of a colorful library shelf or a red-brick schoolhouse.

Before I'd even finished telling them about Mumbai, my mother declared, "Well, I'm glad *that* trip is done at last."

"Are you?" I glared at her as my father stirred his Sanka.

"Look," she explained. "It all doesn't have to be so, so—"

"Flighty," my father helped her out reluctantly.

"Yes," she agreed, rotating the plastic creamer on the side table in a nervous rhythm. "It's just, we worry."

"Well, stop." The stiff exchange of people who all know that no one will be swayed but feel obligated to go through the motions anyway; everyone just wants to make nice—so they could live with themselves that they tried, and so I could live with myself that I let them.

"A mother never stops. Talia, you know that, too. We just want to help. You're in your head all the time, so restless, and then you come out with such strangeness. Even this divorce. You were perfectly fine for years and years and then suddenly you tell us everything is broken." She said this for the twentieth time, but as if she was revealing something new and disturbing. "And the way you talk about it, making jokes. I know you think you're being funny, but it's odd. I mean, are you depressed again, is that it?"

"Rina..." My father cut in, trying to cushion it.

"What?" she turned to him. "It could be true, you know that." She sighed and then turned back to me. "We just want you to settle down, get married again, and rebuild your life."

Even my father nodded now, apologetic, but agreeing.

"Tell me," I huffed. Why, unfailingly whenever I was around them, did I start to act like a child again? I lowered my voice, trying to speak more evenly. "What else do *you* want out of *my* life?"

I pushed back my chair and took my barrel of coffee outside onto the porch, trying not to storm out like a child, but the way an adult would. They followed a few minutes later.

"Since when do you drink coffee?" my mother asked, bringing out a pie to go with it. A gesture of peace.

"Actually, this is my very first one."

"Well, good grief and hallelujah!" my father declared from behind her, as if this proved something. "If that's not better already, then nothing is."

We laughed and softened, and as we sat on the bench I told them about meeting Philip on the plane ride home and his suggestion that I teach this semester.

My father lit up. "You always *were* good with an audience. Even that time you finished the semester for me."

I grimaced. "I had no business teaching a class on folklore."

"It was a bit of a stretch, sure. But you were fine." He nodded his head vehemently. "Especially considering you had a small kid at home. No time to prepare. You made it your own. More creative writing than theory, sure, but the students seemed to get a lot out of it. A college could be a good place for you. Plus all that interest with your play. Remember that panel you did?"

My mother could not stop nodding. "What luck, to have a teaching position just offered to you. With academia as crazy as it is these days… Remember that college in New Hampshire?" She turned to my father and then back to me. "You were little, but your father used to teach at this college when we lived in Boston, and he'd drive all the way up there. It was a special place. Earnest professors, all hard workers. And one year, kind of as an experiment, the administration handed everything over to the faculty. It was going to be some sort of utopia. It was going to be what education was always meant to be."

"Well, what happened?" I asked.

"It was wonderful at first," my father explained. "One time, three different departments needed a new hire but there was only funding for two positions. Now, ordinarily, you'd have a fight to the death between departments and administration. But in this case, the three department chairs sat down and discussed each department's needs in order to learn which really required it immediately. And that was how they made the decision. It was all very civilized."

"So the experiment was a success?" I looked from one to the other.

"Well," my father admitted reluctantly, "things changed. Keeping the Board and donors happy, and handling the business of it was bigger than a group of professors with bright intentions. The college ran itself into the ground about five years ago and had to close. Luckily, I was out by then. But if it had worked, that would have been something."

There was a morose silence as my parents took the opportunity to lament all the cycles that had pushed their lives this way, then that. It was a regular exercise and debate for them: the mortgage that fell through, the investment that should have happened, the move to Israel and back, and the academic market.

But then my mother brightened. "At least there's a job for *you*."

She nodded at my father to confirm it. Knowing her so well, I could see she wanted to say something after that, but then she checked herself and made the unusual effort to hold her tongue. She fidgeted uncomfortably, wrung her hands a couple of times, and then quickly gave it up, blurting out, "I hope this guy Philip is not one of these loonies you're always finding, though." My father gave her the eye. "No matter. Look, it's a job. You'll still keep freelancing, of course. But that was never going to be enough…now that you're all alone. And this is a proper job. How could you possibly say no?"

"I'm still thinking about it," I tried to say with finality. But she had a point and I let it sink in. It could be good, really good, to be a professor. *Professor.* The word itself sounded exhilarating. I said it over a couple of times in my head, sliding deliberately over a lingering, affected *o* sound.

Academia was enticing to me, and not just because the sparseness of semesters and summer vacation and reclusive office hours lined up rather well with my dislike for attachment. It was more than that. It was a chance to inhabit literature, to become alive through stories. Left to myself, I always preferred to dwell in their midst over anything real, aside from Aiden.

My parents could tell I was starting to come over to their thinking. "Well," my mother exhaled, "it's decided then."

They were grateful to hear of this prospect of stability, so certain that, naturally, everyone *would* desire it. They both sighed in relief. After I left, they would replay every little part of the conversation again and eventually launch a new round of worries. But for now at least they had a bit of calm. So they cut generous pieces of pie, and we all clutched little plates of it and ate as if we were celebrating.

3.

I called Philip the next day. "I'm yours," I told him. I pieced together a syllabus and some paperwork and dug up some old copies of my play and my resume for Human Resources. I even took out Jack's old coffee machine, plugged it in on the counter and bought a box of 300 coffee pods with one of the grocery store coupons that I myself had written.

The day before classes started, I met Philip on campus. First he introduced me to the dean, a perpetually frowning woman in gray. "Talia's working on a new play," he lied as we stood in the doorway of her office.

The woman brightened. "The board will love that—multiculturalism is what's bringing in all the grants these days."

I received a faculty code for the printer machines, to Xerox my syllabi. I smoothed a Staff Lot sticker onto my windshield. And just like that, as if gifted by the Wizard of Oz, I was a professor. I had my own audience and forum, my own small channel back to the beloved writers who first inspired me, whose stately gilded books passed through my childhood under flashlight and bed covers, whose characters seemed to live more than I ever could. I was awed at officially being a part of some academic authority that I had once associated with the seeming-perfection that was my father, and that had impressed me when I was a student myself, on the small-desk side of the college classroom.

New plays or books, critically acclaimed bestsellers, could be written from this new place, just like Philip had suggested to the dean—if I got my act together. Students could be inspired to read and write them, too. Everything seemed possible now as I pictured myself coaxing wisdom from my students, holding some bit of mystical Socratic power in my palm.

Philip and I walked through the quad, a quaint brick square with a stretch of grass in the center, and classrooms and offices all around. The faculty building, Nevis Hall, at one time had been a student dorm and the offices still had that look of stacked, uniform rooms, littered with bulletin boards and photos and the odd twin bed here and there. Philip stopped in at one of the first offices, rapping loudly on the door. "This is Sebastian," he introduced. "Incoming department chair to replace me—thank goodness. Revered authority on the seventeenth century. And on Joyce. And," he pointed to a corner of the room where the big man kept several warehouse-sized bags of candy, "on all things piggish."

"Welcome." Sebastian seemed unfazed, opening a chocolate bar, and gesturing at the giant bags with a mild wave. "Anytime you want it, my sweets are your sweets."

We continued the tour. Philip pointed out his own office, the bathrooms, and faculty kitchen, and then stopped before the door at the end of the hall. "This, darling, is your very own office." He opened the door and turned on the light. There was a desk, swivel chair, and couch, and a Metallica poster still pasted in the closet. "It's dusty, I know, and that poster must be twenty years old. Sorry about that."

"Are you kidding?" I put my bags down. "Don't be sorry for anything. You've saved me." I turned to him and clutched my chest, choked up a moment, feeling grateful that the gaping hole always nearby for years and years seemed a bit further off. "For now, anyway."

He looked at me knowingly. "If—when—you need to go searching again for God or some other bologna, you don't have to get on a plane to somewhere crazy. Try getting laid locally. That should do it. Or, try coming here." I followed him, puzzled, to the back of the office where it turned sharply into a windowed alcove, large enough to almost be its own room. "This is *my* wisdom," he explained, pointing to several tall stacks of books in one corner.

I crouched to read along the spines. "Cookbooks are your wisdom?" I frowned. "I know you make a living from it, but it's just food, you know."

He tisked. "Food is the first and last cult. Human history rises and falls over bread."

"Here and now though, we live a life of plenty." I thought of the bustling Quarter as I had seen it the other morning. "Many of us do, anyway. And I should know: I write the coupons for it." I shrugged and ran one finger over a faded Julia Child cover, thinking of the campers on field trip at the museum the other day. "Anyway, if you are one of those people who have all you want, and clearly you are," I looked at him pointedly, almost in accusation, "then why the fuss?"

"That's exactly what I'm saying." He spread his hands triumphantly, as if I had just proved his point. "There is no good reason for how we live and eat other than our collective insanity."

I followed him out of the alcove into the office. "Insanity, because why else would anyone use butter like we use butter?"

"There you go!" He laughed out loud. "Next time you're lost, I'm going to save you." He held up two soft hands, like an evangelical. "Food is going to save you." He curled the fingers of both hands together, searching for words. "We don't eat just to survive anymore, we eat to transcend. Food is a living thing now, really. Like music in the 1960s."

"Consider the feast." Philip proclaimed. He brought a bottle of wine from his office and opened it now. While I cleaned shelves and arranged furniture, he got drunk. "Consider Juliette's. And Couchon," he raved, writing the names of restaurants and markets I needed to try on tiny yellow post-its that he stuck all over my walls. "And the recent wave of moonshine cocktails. And this new thing they're doing with octopus. And a place upstate at an orchard—I'll get the name for you. Also, when I come back from LA, I'll take you to The Quarter, parts you've never seen when you go to your little market."

"How do you know what I've seen?"

He ignored me. "And Prongs, of course! Definitely Prongs." I borrowed a broom from the kitchen and tidied up as he told me about the night he camped out for fresh cropiedos and about all the Food Show stars he'd dated, men mostly but some women too, just for a change. Eventually, Philip staggered down the hall to his office, gesturing with one thumb back to the alcove of books. "You'll be born again," he promised.

––––––––––

The next morning, Philip flew to Los Angeles to teach a month-long senior seminar at the west coast campus as he oversaw editing of the archeological footage. I was left alone to meet my students. They'd been gradually moving on campus all week, but now they sprouted everywhere as I walked through the quad, a swarm of punky bodies.

In one corner they played rap. In another corner, a cluster of boys who had their own death metal band perched on the wall, carefully listening to their recording from last year at the bar on Folsom entertaining a few drunken locals. This was just the start of their story, they told each other, early days at college before making it big. This would be where it all began.

Two girls—new lovers who had met at orientation—held hands nonchalantly to make a public statement about not needing to make a public statement. They laughed too loudly over something, and then carefully looked to see if they'd been noticed.

On the other side of them, a couple of upperclassmen, who had been inseparable last year but had broken up over the summer, experimented with awkward small talk, oblivious to everything else in their square of misery. He still relived how he'd messed it up; she still held hostage the sweatshirt they'd bought in Maine, which smelled, deliriously, like him.

Everywhere, large groups of students were busy in conversation, upperclassmen reuniting, first-years talking about how long ago high school already seemed to be and tallying how much they'd drunk last night, part fine-tuned bragging, part weary, feigned regret.

One girl walked by with an enormous violet butterfly tattooed on her chest. Another student caught up to her, carefully defiant with the thick scars that cuffed his wrists and golden earlobe rings. By the time they brushed past me, heading late into the humanities building, there was a pack of them, all well-fed and uninhibited and ironic.

My first classes went smoothly that day and I was feeling more at ease when I arrived to teach my last class, Creative Writing. It was still early and so I set up the chairs. Students filtered in as I handed out copies of the syllabus and signed add-drop slips. Just as I was closing the door to begin, one last student slipped through the door.

She was a beautiful girl, but in a strange way, like a cartoon drawing, with banged hair that was the color of ginger. It fell to her shoulders in bandy swoops, and she had luminous black eyes and that blue-white skin that is not so fashionable now but was, for centuries, royal. Even as she walked to her desk, she seemed to be a sensual creature, aware of her body moving and swaying. She was fully steeped in it, almost to the point of being flamboyant. It was there in everything she did.

But there was also intelligence behind her sexuality, a keen sense of subtext. Something about her—so ripe with potential, so driven by whims and affected by glances—set her apart from those who should have been her peers. But they weren't her peers; that was clear. She was unusual somehow, with a casual recklessness that suggested that even she did not understand the value, or the danger, in it. And even as I cleared my throat to speak to the class, I found her to be alarming and unpredictable, as if she might stand up in class for no reason and shout, or left to her own devices, she might bring a first-edition Gutenberg Bible for the sole purpose of bathroom reading, or dance blithely along a precarious cliff-edge till the footing crumbled away. She seemed much bolder than I had ever been when I was young, but the way she was oblivious to events and circumstances that would surely come along and change everything that she thought she knew reminded me of my younger self.

Stumbling over the words, I introduced myself to the class and then went through the attendance chart until I reached her name:

Penny Mallow, a senior. The girl half-raised her hand. She barely looked forward as she discreetly peeled an orange, one by one sucking off each section, her gauzy tank top and stringy straps sliding along her skin and baring body parts with every move. I took a deep breath. At least I knew her name.

I introduced the syllabus and answered questions about the schedule, finding a rhythm as I spoke, pacing at the front of the class, then planting my feet and making a few jokes. I gave the students an assignment to work on for ten minutes in class, and when they were finished, I asked them to revise it and hand it in at our next meeting. Finally, I dismissed them, and collecting my books, made my way back to my office. Standing in the alcove, I looked out over the quad, decompressing from the day, daring, almost, to congratulate myself. A couple of bumps, but it had been a pretty good start.

Then I saw her, Penny Mallow, slinking through the crowd. I pressed against the window. Where was she going? She seemed to be heading toward the pond at the center of the quad. Other students were clustered there too, sitting along the short wall around it, enjoying the sun. But Penny Mallow wasn't joining a group, she went straight for an empty stretch of wall, where she threw down her books, slipped off her sandals and jacket, pulled her shirt and bra off over her head, and lay down on the wall to sun herself, wearing jeans and nothing else.

What was she thinking? How long would she stay like that? I could not draw myself away from the window, nearly breathless from both intrigue and bother. Some students stopped and pointed, some did not. But Penny was oblivious to them all, like a stage performer trained to play to the audience, without ever seeing them or breaking character.

Nearly fifteen minutes later, one of the campus security guards approached and spoke to her at length. Though I could not hear the exchange, he was clearly becoming exasperated. Eventually, lazily, Penny stood up, put on her sandals, and collected her books. She looped her jean jacket over one shoulder and walked away, still topless.

I watched until she disappeared through the parking lot across the quad. Only then did I back away from the window, bumping into Philip's pile of cookbooks. The books tumbled heavily around me. I knelt to stack them again, lingering over the last one in my hands, a worn copy of *The Joy of Margo Sesame.* I started to leaf through it.

The book was dog-eared, smudged with oil, dusty with flour, and pocked with Philip's professorial margin notes. I took it to read on the couch. Professors, I imagined, knew how to cook and eat with gusto. My father's pallid example long ago didn't count because other than teaching the odd class here and there, he mostly did research. But professors, *real* professors who were stars and in the thick of it, ate well and in hearty company. Once in a while, they might get caught up in a week-long debate on some fragment of Welsh folktale and forget to eat. And in that case, they would live on tea from an electric kettle in their office. But when life settled down again they would age their own beef and make fresh cornbread. And they would invite over their witty friends who were doing important things and set out heaping wooden bowls of salad from their gardens, and drink the red wine brought in cases each year from their favorite vineyard.

When I'd finished browsing through it, I returned to the alcove and added Margo Sesame's book to the pile. The next book was a cookbook devoted to candying, and I took that back to the couch. I closed my office door and read that book too, studying each glossy photo and recipe, start to finish, throughout the empty afternoon, and losing the day to candy land.

"To get to know each other," I told my Creative Writing class next day, "I'd like each of you to write a paragraph about yourselves. And then, a *confession.*"

They scribbled silently for a while and then each student took a turn reading what he had written. Most of the stories were not-un-expected college age confessions, still steeped in soft privilege, which sorely needed to be singed away so that they might someday actually begin to live and write. I reassured wary students: you can say what you want here.

When it was Penny's turn, she began to read, and I heard her voice clearly for the first time. It sounded younger than I had expected, throaty and fried and lilting with questions even when she wasn't asking, but stating something. Still, it was precise and unapologetic.

She read through her own clichés, how she had worked her way through most of her college years as, predictably, a stripper. Several months before this semester, her last, she had left that job for one of her clients, a fifty-something CEO named Donald. He had taken her to Mexico, then last month to Italy. They shopped together. He chose lingerie for her, and she chose dapper, hipster suits for him from high-end consignment shops in the village. Orange hats and cowboy boots that were ironic on a man his age, but fun, so she laughed, and then they laughed together. Donald paid for everything she wanted and needed and did not mind if she had young boyfriends as long as she was available to him 'round the clock and up for anything—which, she assured us, was always the case anyway. She wanted to be a writer when she grew up, she told us, and the senior thesis she was working on would be a collection of original poetry on the life and times of a stripper. "It's called *Stiletters*," she said in a deadpan.

But none of this was her confession. Instead, at the very end she admitted this: "My short fiction won second place in *Frontiers*. It was about a girl and her boyfriend doing it in the public bathroom at his daughter's Bat Mitzvah party, while his wife yelled at the caterer in the other room. But," she told us, "it wasn't fiction at all; it was true."

And this, she announced crisply to the students—not the adultery, or the pudgy Bat Mitzvah girl, Donald's daughter, who cried because she guessed—was the literary lie that made her ashamed. Fact for fiction, fiction for fact: that was her confession.

I returned to my office after class, still thinking of Penny and trying to absorb what I had heard, the mixture of plain-speak and defiance, and a tinge of fatigue edging in that she probably didn't even yet know she felt. Where would she be in ten years? Maybe living somewhere down the road, in town, with a husband and three children and a retail job. She would probably be wearing sensible 'mom pants,' like me. Time would have lined its way onto her face, sealing her off each year in a life that was, quite possibly, dreary. And that brief window she'd thrown open to the world during college, would have shown only a brilliant flash that faded even before it started, because she was so damn sure she had it all figured out.

I leaned against my desk, brushing against the candy cookbook taken from the pile on the day before, brilliant confectionary colors of cherry and ginger and maple on its cover. I looked at it thoughtfully. Then, on a whim, I grabbed my car keys and drove to the Channing grocery store a mile off campus.

Commuters were leaving campus for the evening when I came back to my office with several shopping bags. I brought my groceries to the small kitchen, where dorm students had once mulled over ramen. Rummaging the shelves, I pushed past old roach traps, mismatched plates and forks, and a bag of shot glasses collected during spring break somewhere. Finally, I discovered three small pots and several thick spoons.

I turned the stove knob, listening to the old pipes creak and ache, then click, then light. When the rings were hot enough, I boiled sugar and butter till they thickened and made candied apricots and nuts, candied lemon slices and onions and pumpkin seeds. When each batch was done, I poured it to cool into some old glass jelly jars that I'd found on a shelf above the fridge. When I finally sat down, mopping the sweat from my forehead, it was just after midnight.

I hadn't noticed the time passing and suddenly I was hungry. The foods I had made were scattered across my moonlit office surfaces, like coins pulled from the ocean. I took a beer from Philip's office and picked at the glistening spread before me. Afterwards, dishes spanned the sink and counter, a snowfall of ceramic shapes. A tiny plate congealed with splashes of yolky sugar water. Forks encrusted in the impossible spaces between the prongs. There was also a wide white soup bowl stained unforgivingly by curry from years ago now full of seed shells. I turned on the water and used a cup of hand soap from the bathroom to scrub, starting as always with the big flat dishes first as they seemed to take up the most space. I lined them up, steaming and nestled onto each other like sleeping lovers. Then the silverware—a fistful of forks, then spoons together, then knives, each one scrubbed alone. Then spatulas and pots.

After cleaning up, I fell asleep on my couch, slumped over in my clothes. I had to go to class in the morning with a jacket over me, to hide yesterday's wrinkled clothes. But the next time I was more prepared. And when I drove from home the following day, I brought a small suitcase of clothes. I looped my toiletries and suit hanger on the hook behind the office door, tossed a sleeping bag and pillow onto the couch, and unpacked a few extra pots and pans. And so, during those first few weeks of school, on the nights when Aiden stayed at Jack's and I didn't want to make the lonely drive home, this was my home, and my lab, of sorts.

Each night, I set out to cook one food or another, fermenting, infusing, pickling, making cider. And while most professors were at home with their families, I was, in between grading papers, puttering around the kitchen in that abandoned building with my sweat pants and slippers, tending simmering pots and boiled jars.

One night as I cooked, the campus guard, Parker, stuck his head into the kitchen. "What's going on in here?" he asked.

"This?" I emerged from behind an enormous ball of sourdough. "I guess this looks a bit strange, huh?"

He watched me, straight-faced. "Not gonna lie to you."

"I'm Philip's new hire," I tried to reassure him.

His eyes narrowed. "Craziness happening here at all hours. Students sexing up the common room. Bunch of cars got keyed last night."

"You like bread?" I offered him a still-hot roll. He chewed it thoughtfully, surveying the floury tabletop for a moment. Eventually, deciding I was harmless enough, he left me to my work.

The more I dabbled in Philip's wisdom—food—the more I became awed by it. This was not the same food I'd encountered while writing coupons, bulk-packaged and flash-frozen, or buy one get one free. This was not plain, useful food.

This was a craft—relying on sensibility, like that of a skilled fisherman who could read the water and know how far to let out the line exactly and what a certain tug on it meant from a thousand varieties of other tugs. Those insights could only be learned from callouses and dirty hands and so much repetition that the patterns rose, eventually, to the surface. This food was also alchemy in channeling the life force of yeast, in transforming chemistry with a simple egg, in enchanting heat into bubbles and steam. It was a patient mastery of nature and instinct.

Philip phoned from Los Angeles a couple days before returning. "Are you surviving?" he asked. I told him about my cooking experiments. "More when I'm home; I've got to run now. Of course you're coming to my dinner party…" He hung up before I could ask or answer.

I kissed Aiden goodbye as he slept and drove to school in the early morning hours so I could grade papers before class. Stopping at the old donut shop outside Beacon, I chose a pumpkin pie donut with my iced coffee and nursed it as I drove down the back roads.

The final turn before campus was a strange sweet road that seemed to be the very last country road for hundreds of miles. A team of horses pulling a wagon turned from a dirt path onto the street so I slowed down behind it. On either side of me, as the sun rose, the land rolled open in strokes of green splashed with duck-dotted ponds and red wooden grain silos. Through the car windows, it was seamless, like a painting in a children's book of farmland, no brown patches in the green, no chipped paint on the walls, only fresh manure dropped unceremoniously by the horses in front of me, its scent filtering in from the air vents.

I drove through the Channing gates, past a small fenced forest and then behind the main academic quad. I parked in the faculty lot and turned off the car. Suddenly the coffee high drained out of me and I felt a sinking feeling again, the suspicion which always overtook me eventually, that despite all that seemed good, something was wrong.

I headed to my office with an armful of stuff from the back of my car. Every day when I walked into the faculty building, it seemed that I discovered new vestiges from its time as a student dorm. Early on it had been cavernous showers in the basement, and a common room television with an old-time wire antenna. Today it was a Spring Gala poster glued behind the stairwell—never ripped down, never painted over—for April 12, 1997.

I walked to the alcove window in my office to see how my recipes had fared over the last few days. The sill and the bookshelf that cornered it had become my makeshift pantry. It was a magnificent spread of mason jars and cans, tall bottles holding liquids of every color, sealed tin boxes and a small refrigerator that I asked Parker to bring up from the basement, plugged in below, with cheeses and lemons and cream.

I surveyed last week's pickles that lined the windows in bright, cleanly labeled splendor. There were jars of pickled hard-boiled eggs, pickled lemon, pickled herring. There was bright orange kimchi and pickled beets, olives and sweet tiny cucumbers. I took one of the jars of pickled cucumbers and brought it to my desk. There was yogurt in the refrigerator, too, for lunch. I flipped on the computer and sat down at my desk chair, settling into the familiar gaps of cracked leather.

I had probably been immersed in grading papers for at least an hour when suddenly I looked up and saw Penny Mallow peeking through my door. Startled, I tipped my coffee. "Sorry I scared you," she said as I mopped it up. "I didn't think there was anyone in this office."

"No problem." I was flustered. We had never before spoken outside of class. "Were you looking for me?"

She shook her head. "Dr. Aaronson."

"I think he's upstairs."

"Well," she hemmed, "I'm sorry again about the coffee."

"No, it was me," I finally smiled, a bit red in the face, feeling foolish. "I can be a bit of a klutz, I guess."

She looked at me disbelievingly, with her head to one side, as if she were seeing me for the first time, as if this had never occurred to her, that a professor should have some human characteristic like clumsiness, or a past, or plans for the weekend.

Penny frowned slightly and wandered back down the hallway. And I shook my head, admonishing myself. *Of course* she could not imagine beyond the immediacy of student life. *Of course* she would see all her professors in weathered anonymity. Such obliviousness was half the joy and intensity of college.

That evening, for the first time, I was restless in my office. I spent a few hours making chili pastes. Afterward, I was brushing my teeth for the night and dawdled a moment at the sink of the darkened faculty bathroom. Suddenly, I caught sight of myself in the green glow of the mirror. I saw myself, as if through someone else's eyes, still wearing my bun from the day and looking restless. What the hell was I really doing there anyway, digging through Philip's old cookbooks night after night?

I went back to my office and took out the thick packet of brown-paper labels. *Chili paste with lime,* I wrote in neat marker, and then pressed it, glue-side down, to the newly filled jar. *Sweet Thai chili paste,* I wrote on the next label. By the time all the jars were labeled and packed away, I had almost forgotten my ghost in the mirror.

I was just drifting off to sleep on my couch when I heard voices down the hall. I sat straight up at once. Who else was here? No one was ever here at night. No one but me.

I grabbed a frying pan off the shelf by my door, armed as if in a Bugs Bunny cartoon. I crept down the corridor toward the noise. The room that was once the student common room was lit up, and it seemed to be snowing in there, tiny white flurries moving through stale air. I squinted, trying to make sense of it. Strangest of all, Parker, the security guard with his flashlight and security uniform, was shouting and sneering, shaking his head at Penny Mallow.

And I saw now that it wasn't actually snowing. But some of the old couches had been slashed and the musty feathers, after being packed inside the cushions for decades, had been released into the air and were floating everywhere.

Parker saw me and pointed to the gaping wounds in the couch. "Look here, professor. This is the same kid who's been making trouble all over campus. I saw a bunch of them come in here. The rest ran off, but at least she's left."

"It wasn't me." She stared at him coldly.

"Yeah, right," he told me. "I've caught her trying to sneak into faculty offices during Finals. And last year, someone threw a couple of melons off the observatory roof one night. A few people said it was her, but she wormed her way out of it." He shook his head. "But not this time."

"It wasn't me," she said again and then turned to me. "You believe me, don't you, professor? I swear it."

"No making nice now." Parker sniggered. "This time you're out of here."

Something in this suddenly struck Penny as real, and she paled as he quickly crossed the room and advanced on her. She was wild-haired and heroin thin, maybe a bit drunk, with one of her bra straps loose again. As he closed in on her, he had that look I had sometimes seen men give when they came across a young woman, reeking of damage—that rising snarl of desire and power.

"Actually," I cleared my throat, "she was with me, Parker."

He stopped in his tracks. "At this hour?"

"We were going over some notes."

"For my senior thesis," Penny added, coming closer to me. From her backpack she pulled out a messy pile of papers previously stuffed into a manila folder. "She's on my committee."

"I suppose the kids you heard running off were responsible for this." I nodded toward the exit. "You can probably still catch them if you go now."

He looked knowingly at the frying pan in my hand, then back at me, then at Penny, and muttering under his breath, he walked out the door. "This one is on you, professor."

The last of the snow feathers had settled now and I turned to

Penny. "Follow me." We walked silently down the hall toward my office. I was already regretting this. Sure, I was mesmerized by her. Sure, I was also scared for her, a mess and careening toward self-destruction. But my mothering instincts had taken over, and now, it seemed, I was stuck with her.

I turned on the light inside my office and closed the door behind us.

"I didn't do it," she said in the coy deliberate voice I had come to know from class.

"Yes, you did," I told her sharply. "How many times has this kind of thing happened? No, actually," I interrupted myself, "don't answer. I don't want to know."

"Are we done here?" She turned to me coolly. It was the same air of privilege: I want what I want when I want it, with a quick and presumptuous irritation lingering just below the practiced surface of control.

"Say the word, and I'll let Parker take you straight to the Dean. I'm the only one trying to help you here." I thought quickly, and then made a decision. "Until you graduate this semester, I'm going to have my eye on you. And I am going to be on your thesis committee. You're going to get your act together, or Parker can finish this."

"Fine." In answer to my challenge, she tossed the manila folder full of her thesis drafts onto my desk. Then she opened her hands flat in front of me, as a show of surrender. Inside one palm lay the razor she had used to slash the couch. "Fair enough," she added, "given the circumstances."

4.

The next day, early, I was still sleeping off the strange events from last night, when Philip stuck his head through the crack in the door. I gave him a bear hug and led him into the alcove to sit where he saw the full spread of shelves and the wall of my preserves. He laughed out loud, but shook his head, too, looking me over in my pajamas and the splayed open sleeping bag. "Leave it to you to turn it into *this*."

I heated some bone broth for him to taste. "How is it?" I asked.

"Not bad." He sipped, gripping the mug with two hands. Then he sat at the edge of my desk in between papers and jars of kimchi to tell me all about Los Angeles, class and film editing, and a washed up model he had gone out with a few times. "The more washed up they are, the more eager," he explained.

"You're impossible." Nothing made Philip happier than a bit of the twisted. He winked, as if he had been kidding, but even then I knew he was actually serious, in his free-fall way, where nothing was unacceptable. And just as I had several times since returning to academia, where everything was relative and politically correct and pastel, I wondered fleetingly how faint the line could be between owning something and being owned by it. "That's it." I stood up and opened the door. "I'm afraid I have to kick you out now. Didn't you see the sign, No Nasty Old Men here?"

"I must have missed that." He rose and glided to the door. "No matter. We can take this up again at my party tonight." He offered a smile. "Excited?"

I nodded. "And a little scared."

"Don't be scared. None of the people I know are half as wicked as me."

I taught a section of Composition and then returned to my office. Settling behind my desk, I started to leaf through Penny's folder for the first time, wondering what this would be, this poetry about stripping. I scanned the pages slowly at first, then more quickly. The showiness of it left me with a kind of bewilderment. It had promise, but was completely off in the tone, vapid, so it also left me with the hair standing up on my arms. *High heels of a giant. Naked thighs, fingers, lies.* Who was this girl?

I shook it off and as evening descended drove to Philip's house. It was strange and new, to go to a party alone, after so many years of being married. The car felt empty now as I mulled over the logistics, where once each part of the pair had had a role—Jack carrying the jackets, me carrying the hostess gift—and always there had been someone to cross the room to, if needed.

Philip's neighborhood lay on the other side of the city, on the far side of The Quarter. It was an exclusive neighborhood, private security cars patrolling the streets, and it looked like Early America, with stately brick brownstones, drapes of ivy, odd pieces of road still paved in old cobblestone, and an antiquated streetlamp now and then. I parked under a vast Copper Beech, touching a hand to its thick elephant skin bark as I walked past. Around me, the quiet evening sounded of small clinks from screened windows and a faint breeze sighing now and then. I walked up Philip's porch steps and rang the bell.

"What are you waiting for?" Philip opened the front door at once, pressing a tall glass of punch into my hand. "You should drink."

I took a sip of cold strawberry sour and followed him into the living room. High ceilings of stained glass and gold-crusted paintings crowned the place. A large crystal punch bowl sat upon a table at the center of the room. A long couch curved around it, with several people including Sebastian, the new head of the English department, squashed into the bend of the cushions.

"Look who it is now." Sebastian waved me over, happily drunk behind a platter of canapés.

I moved to sit with him, but Philip pulled me past. "No, no. Not by the hobbit."

"Hush," I hissed.

"What?" He shrugged matter-of-factly. "Sebastian knows he's a hobbit. Everyone knows he's a hobbit."

I looked out of the corner of my eye at him. It was true. Sebastian *was* a bit of a hobbit, porky and white-haired—a good-natured glutton. "But do you need to say it so rudely?"

"It's for his own good. He needs to hear it."

I watched Sebastian over my shoulder. He seemed unbothered by the remark, slurping the next piece of smoked salmon into his mouth with gusto. But that was their way, as far as I could tell, with Philip delivering barbs about his appetite, and Sebastian enjoying the cruelty.

Philip led me to the far end of the couch. "This is better. I like my ladies lined up in a row." He seated me near an adjunct professor from the Women's Studies department who was perched stiffly in a suit on the edge of her seat. "You've probably met Ruth. Also, do you know Alison?" Philip pointed to the girl on the other side of me. She wore a long trailing ball gown and was probably nineteen.

"You look familiar." I tried to place her. "Are you one of Philip's students?"

"Yes. I also live here." She pointed upstairs.

Philip bent down to speak to her quietly, and they both laughed about something. Ruth raised her eyebrows. "Did she just say what I think she said?"

"Yes," I admitted. "But you know Philip." I tried to cover for him. "I'm sure it's innocent, mostly."

"And so appropriate," she drawled, shaking her head.

She sat up squarely in her corner of the couch and glared at him, indignant and proper. Philip did not notice. He lit a fat cigar and straightened his bowtie, then put on some jazz and capered around the room, welcoming the other guests with more punch. Her angry looks dissolved into the air when he did not notice them. He was defiant, or perhaps so confident from how he charmed his way through the world that he was oblivious to any limitation.

His leather shoes skated over the floor, in three-steps and smart turns and jaunty bows so that everyone soon was watching and smiling, including me, and eventually including Ruth. If not from his charm, there was also a parade of brilliant liquids, gushes of amber and running glass and cherry-colored wine that took away the mind and mellowed the body muscle by muscle.

Ruth settled into the cushions. Someone walked by with a few new bottles of wine and she plucked a couple of them out of his arms and sat back to drink, holding a bottle in one hand and her glass in the other. "I'll take some of that." I shrugged and offered her my glass. And by chance seating, Ruth and I discovered a fleeting fellowship, as sometimes happens at parties, when the concentrated time and strangers encourages even the most unlikely connection.

The crowd circled around us. Because we were so near the punch bowl and in possession of bottles, we filled peoples' glasses and chatted with whomever passed. Ruth told me about an article she'd published in *The Chronicle*, recounting excitedly each exchange and blow-by-blow in the volley back and forth with her editor; this footnote and that study were somehow breathless plot points in her adventure story. She introduced me to an artist-in-residence from another local university. I spoke to a woman, who, after a few minutes, I began to suspect was Philip's project before me. She'd grown up in Gibraltar, or maybe Spain. And she had the casual allure of Europeans. Dark haired, fairy boned, with just lipstick, and no bra but a perfectly draped scarf. She had a glass of the punch in her hand and every time she sipped, the silver bracelets jangled on her wrist.

"What's my fantasy?" Ruth asked, slurring just a little, as she refilled my glass again. "I've been teaching adjunct for over twenty years, each year hoping for a promotion, or at least a bit of recognition. Now that I've been published in *The Chronicle*, the president will have to offer me the full-time position that's open."

The evening progressed in slow-motion minutia now.

The Chair of the math department came out of the bathroom with a ribbon of toilet paper attached to his foot. Because I had never liked math, I said nothing. Maybe, no one else had liked math either, because he walked around that way all night long.

A woman sitting nearby had a connect-the-dot tattoo down her leg, which was draped invitingly over a fat ottoman. A young man came by. "Hey," he said, like it was a novel idea, "do you ever let people connect the dots?" Coyly, she produced a magic marker from her purse. They leaned in together, watching line-by-line as he formed the shape down her leg—of a woman with a tattoo down her leg.

A beautiful couple sat in the corner, mostly made beautiful because the woman was, as is often the case, breathtaking to his just-fine. But he seemed to be important, graying in luxurious waves and smelling of powerful cologne. He glanced at his watch now and then. She was twined through his hair and limbs, her fingers meshing with his, and drinking from his glass, so that even their mouths would taste the same.

A drunk, young man—washed-out looking, like he never left the house—lorded over a card table. "I think he's related to Philip somehow," Ruth said. "Maybe his long-lost son…" The man pushed back the table and stood, his thin frame a shadow of Philip's. He went to find a new bottle of gin. "And the guy he's playing with?" She gestured with her chin at another man at the table, dark and chain-smoking. "Someone claimed that he's an exiled journalist. Or an exiled prince. Or maybe both?"

Deep into my next glass of wine, my stomach started to plead hollow sounds. There was no food to be found. I looked for Sebastian's plate of canapés but it was just grease and crumbs on a side table. Ruth, thoroughly gone by that point too, gave a furtive look at the people around us and then said something very quietly from the corner of her mouth, with extravagant stealth.

"What's that? I can't hear you."

She cupped one hand at my ear and enunciated carefully, as if relaying a life and death message. "There's a rumor," her breath was heavy with wine, "about crackers."

I looked around. "I don't see crackers."

She nodded deeply and gave my back a small, encouraging pat, entrusting me with a mission. "Go find them for us."

I planted one hand on either side of me and started to rise, but shaky legs gave way and I fell back onto the couch. Nestled once more within the cushion, the ambition faded. We finished off the enormous bowl of punch and ten minutes later someone re-filled it with eggnog.

Everyone got drunker and drunker. Was Philip not planning to serve food? I wondered. "When I'm able to stand again," I finally declared, "I'm going to find Philip and tell him that he must order pizza or something."

At nine o'clock, Philip sent someone out to pick up steaks from the grocery. At eleven o'clock we were seated finally, and just as quickly as she had attached herself to me, Ruth found herself a chair at the other end of the table. The food emerged, the steak perfectly rare, artfully scalloped potatoes, then lamb, then soup, then bitter greens, and then three cakes.

Philip made his way around the table, talking about cumin, checking in with his guests, raving about the farm where he got his vegetables. "Vegetables are the new cocaine, of course," he informed my neighbor matter-of-factly, like it had been proven somehow. "Do me a favor," he said as he reached me. "Tell me how the cake tastes." He slid a dainty plate of pastry studded with soft apples before me.

"You didn't taste it yet?" I bit into the custard center. "Delicious." He watched me like a hawkish auntie.

"I don't like dessert," he informed me. "Or bread. Or meat. I'm mostly vegetarian."

"Really? Are you sure?" I squinted. "You had my bone broth just this morning, you know."

"Oh." He shrugged. "I'll taste any of those experiments in your office. And take you out for ice cream. And feed you steak. But that's just so you let me spend time with you."

I looked at him in disbelief. "And this dinner? Pretty generous for someone who doesn't like to eat."

"Trust me," he cackled, "this is far more for me than for anyone else."

I took another bite of cake. "You're a strange man."

"I am." He acknowledged this and then looked me close in the face. "Come out with me tomorrow? Just us, none of these other people." He gestured at the rest of the room in irritation, like he suddenly wanted them all gone from his house. "Then we can really talk. About how strange I am. About how strange you are. Whatever you want." I started to ask where and when, but he shushed me at once, as if offended that any of his whims would require explanation. "Tomorrow, then."

5.

Fighting a hangover, I returned to campus the next day in time for my morning class. I passed into the complex of academic buildings, took a deep breath and smelled just-trimmed leaves, something baking in the cafeteria, someone smoking pot. The air of campus life soothed my headache.

College, I saw now from a professor's point of view, was a strange place; but I could also take some refuge in that dreamy languor of the rolling manicured lawns, the sprawling architecture, the promise of things to come. There was a comfort in the intimacy and campiness of it all—of people who knew each other from all-night study sessions over mountains of junk food, of dorm mates who wore flannel footie pajamas together, like giant nostalgic babies.

As I walked, I thought about students who presented some puzzle to me in this new world of teaching; but none more so than Penny. Preoccupied with her life, and feeling herself at the center of the universe, she reminded me of myself years ago. The more I read of her thesis poetry, the more I could see that she tried to provoke everyone around her as I'd never had the nerve to do. But she had that same expectation that I'd once known, a false expectation—or at least a convoluted one—that had led me to overshoot my potential and end up on the other side, empty-handed and somehow surprised. In my life, too, there were waves—of artistic calling, of some young love affair—once so promising as I waited, impatiently, for them to tug me toward extraordinary. But in the end, they just washed away, into the empty, flat and anonymous, as waves will.

That raging, boiling part of me that had once been like Penny was long gone. But seeing her in class day after day, and writing comments on her poetry in the margins, I started to want it again, like a salt-craving. What would I do if I had all that fervor once more? I didn't know, but I was certain I would use it well, pull every drop from it. To have it again and to use it wisely would be a kind of redemption for having let it slip away before.

Redemption, I knew, was elusive though: For a while, when Jack and I were fighting all the time, we tried to find something that would give our life together a higher purpose. We toyed with Buddhism first, but it was too heavy. Then we tried biking together, but Jack soon hurt his ankle. Turned out there was a Kabbalah center just a few bus stops away, so we settled on that. And its wisdom helped us to hold on for a while. Then one time, after we argued about fixing something in the house, maybe the plumbing, Jack cornered me as he always did until he got his way, and I let my grudge linger for days, just as I always did, too, until I finally tired of it and gave up and said, "Okay, I'm sorry."

"No, you're not. Not really." Then he quoted the rabbi from the Kabbalah center, pasting pieces together, which he did when it served his purpose. "In order to repent, really repent and have redemption, you have to face that same opportunity for sin in the future, and you need to handle it better. But you wouldn't handle it better, would you?" And, he was right: I would not.

Soon, the Kabbalah did not succeed in distracting us any longer. So we tried doing jigsaw puzzles instead—great big landscapes that sat out for weeks on the dining room table as they took slow, silent shape, one jagged piece at a time; and when they were complete, we sealed them with glue on the back and framed them, as if they represented some unique accomplishment. But even then, there was no redemption for me, not with him.

Away from Jack now, with the vitality of Philip and Penny and all these fresh-faced students around me, I started to wonder whether, perhaps, I really could do things better? Bring about real change instead of always allowing myself to be drained; still and mute. What if I could actually thrive, not just merely exist? What if there really was some redemption, even for the likes of me?

―――――――

After class, I drove back to the city to meet Philip for dinner, still haunted by thoughts of redemption. Returning from the quiet country campus, the city streets felt thick around me. I recognized a scent swirling in between the patchwork of cement and reflective glass. I sniffed, trying to distinguish it. Under the burn of vendor pretzels and steam pipes, it was the smoldering of plans that might have been.

My own plans, because remnants of my other life were all around me: the cafe that used to be a bookstore; the first place where I saw my play bound and sitting on a shelf, regal, like some force outside of me; and that corner where Jack and I had had our second date, when we were still new and coy together. These plans had long ago deflated but were still fused to me, like scabs, so that I almost did not notice them anymore, and instead it was the plans of others that really clotted the air when I looked around.

So many people, hoping for their lucky break, or just a bit of redemption. People selling ads for a website instead of owning the world-famous restaurant that they believed they were meant to have. Two friends seated together at the window in the corner Thai place, feverishly working out a business idea that will, eventually, fail. People trudging to the gym after work, to get on treadmills and sweat for half an hour, racing to be just a bit faster than the person on the next machine over, as if it were meaningful.

I remembered the certainty that I'd once had about the play I wrote, and for some extraordinary path after that, and a sense of purpose that woke me at night before the crying baby did. It had faded long before Aiden came around, but I still could recognize that earnestness and determination in others. I saw it in every corner of the city and it looked familiar to me, intertwined, the way actual memories of a moment and mere photos of that moment, all become one and the same.

"A train station bar is a ballsy thing," I said to Philip, pointing at the crowd crisscrossing near where we sat an hour later. We perched at ease on leather stools that popped up like mushrooms around the bar's perimeter. Nearby, swarms of commuters with their sweaty upper lips and clammy foreheads milled past in a death march. "Everyone's hustling past us. And we're just sitting here, like warlords with our vodka."

"I like that." He raised his glass, tinkling the ice. "To warlords."

I took a deep drink, trying to shake off my gnawing thoughts. "What is this place, anyway?" I looked around. Of course, I had passed it a thousand times over the years, as it was located inside The Quarter's only train station. But this was no ordinary bar.

"Purr is Lena Pott's latest Prongs outpost—more casual, *much* easier to get into, and without all the security and scandal." He pointed down one corridor. "Follow that hallway and you'll get to the street entrance for Prongs. We'll go there soon too, you and me. Meanwhile, we have a bit of it here." He pointed to the interior room, where there was a chocolate cake as big as a small car. "It's a layer of cake followed by a layer of ganache mixed with real gold dust, then cake, then ganache, and so on, all the way up. One hundred layers total. Last time I was here, there was a life-size gingerbread house with stained-glass rock candy windows. Charming, sure, but this is far more grand." He waved a hand. "Go on. Be the first to dig in." Indeed, there was a stack of plates and a chainsaw-sized serving knife by the cake for anyone who dared to cut it. He saw my hesitation. "No? Then maybe dinner."

The waiter sauntered over smartly. "Menus?"

"Let me get this," Philip insisted. He ordered lettuce for himself, dry, but for me, a spread of tapas that he somehow knew by heart from the choices. We talked while I dug into soft morsels of mushroom and plucked stuffed olives off my plate. The whole time, Philip watched me as if in a state of suspense, studying my lips, and my throat as I swallowed. He seemed, as always, to be looking for something, like he was trying to make sense from a heap of human reactions—surprise, pleasure, pucker, gulp—and to catalogue them.

Between plates, we returned to our drinks and watched the bustle around us. Beyond the great cake monolith, Purr spilled over into one corner of the cavernous train station. Going into the other wings, there were the lights of early Christmas decorations and early shopping urgency. In the still ongoing commuter's march, the women wore sneakers and suits, relieved to be out of the high heels that burst their veins all day. The men loosened the ties around their necks as they passed, but left them there still looped, able to muster the strength to go that far but no more.

I watched Philip as he watched them, his face both amused and repulsed. He was a handsome man, even considering his age and baldness. "You've aged well, haven't you? Better than I will," I said suddenly.

"Please. You know you're beautiful."

I had once been beautiful; it was true. And Philip could still use that word on me, unblinking. But I knew the truth. Already I had faint lines on my forehead and parentheses around my mouth from the smiles that grew tighter year after year, more a nod to a smile than an actual smile. I snipped stray gray hairs that haunted my temples when I found them. Some of the weight from pregnancy never fully left but instead made itself at home. My shoulders sagged a little under the weight of thousands of hours of uneasiness—hours and energy stolen from me, from my sleep, from Jack when he was still my husband, and from Aiden's irreplaceable years. Yes, I had once been vibrant. But everything previously fresh and energized in me was now drowned, twisted and wrung out, only still present in shreds of itself. Shaking my head at Philip, I realized I wanted redemption from all this, too.

"But aging is the least of your problems," Philip said to my surprise.

"How's that?"

"I've known you only a month or so? And I love you already, I do. But you've got to get out there and really live."

"I get out—"

"Please," he interrupted.

"I'm out there," I mumbled again, thinking of all my false starts.

Philip shook his head. "You finally get up the nerve to go to India? Then you come right back home with your tail between your legs. You're single again, you start a new job? I keep waiting to hear stories, about a fling or new friends, something. Instead, you just dig down and turn my cookbooks into a barricade." He continued, despite the stunned look on my face. "Maybe you've been this way your whole life, what do I know. But truth is, none of the wisdom in the world will help you if you're a mouse."

"You don't know me." I finished my vodka in one long drink, unnerved that he was saying the exact things that were always on my mind. "You don't."

"Maybe." He looked around a moment, then pointed again at the gorgeous monstrous cake, perfectly frosted and poised, still waiting for someone to walk into the center of the room and slice it. "So go over there. Go cut that cake."

I looked at him, then at the cake, then again at him. "No," I said finally.

"Right." He leaned back and nodded like this confirmed it: redemption or no, I was the obstacle in my own way. "That's what I thought."

6.

A buttery sun bled through the haze next morning, persistent and edging bright behind my closed eyelids. It prodded me in the same raw, uncomfortable way that Philip had the night before, pushing me, double-daring me. I pictured that chocolate cake again—the frosting forming thousands of tiny peaks around its perimeter like dragon-skin, the creamy cocoa perfume that rose from it like breath and possessed the entire room. How had I said no to that cake?

Angry with myself, I got up and showered, letting the water burn down my back as I hid in the steam. But the heat didn't take off the edge.

Out of the shower and brushing my teeth, I wandered out to my desk. A string of photo frames lined its top. There was Aiden, as a baby, then at five, and finally from this past school year, at age fourteen. There was Aiden with my parents, then one of me and Jack and Aiden together, when we were that family. There was JB Picard, whose epic novels I had loved since I was a girl, his photo ripped from a magazine and framed, like I knew him personally, for writing inspiration.

There were a few empty photo frames too, ones we had bought that we never got around to filling with our photos. Instead, they featured placeholder photos of anonymous models. Eventually they became phantoms: a boy fishing; a family at a picnic table. These imposters mimicked who we might have been.

I locked the toothbrush between my teeth and took the photo of the three of us and placed it on Aiden's nightstand instead. Then I took all those empty frames, with that boy fishing and the laughing family—though I felt like I knew them now after all this time—and I threw those in the garbage. I shuffled the remaining frames around, rearranging them so that they suggested a seamless, if revised, history.

I entered the kitchen ready for coffee. Ever since embracing it, coffee had become part of my morning routine, with Jack's old machine my first truck stop of the day. I always selected a pod of the Dark Roast grind in the early morning darkness. I tucked it artlessly into the hollow and pressed a button. When the coffee trickled out, I dumped it over a shovel of sugar and milk, and chugged it once it was cool enough. But this day, staring at Jack's clunky industrial machine, I realized I'd become a coffee drinker in the ugliest sense, maybe worse than my father had been years ago.

Surely there were better ways to drink coffee. Hell, Jack's bean grinder and French Press still hid somewhere in the deepest recesses of the cupboard. If I wished, I could have the beans sent directly from a favorite Colombian plantation, just as Philip did. Maybe grind them fresh every morning and coax out four perfect ounces of espresso, like hatching an egg. And if the taste was not right, I could start over again till it was perfect, head tilted over the grounds studiously, as if trying to read the future in them.

But I did nothing so artful. Instead, as Philip's voice reminded me again in my head: I lived like a mouse. I was a slave, not a king. I was the person who chugged my coffee like a peasant. And I had turned down that magnificent cake. Putting two determined palms flat on the counter, I made a decision. From now on, I would take my coffee like a human being—and I would never again refuse cake.

I swept the roll of coffee pods aside and pulled the coffee machine's plug from the wall. I stuffed the pods and the machine into the garbage bag on top of the empty photo frames. I triple knotted the bag and then placed it into the large container at the curb for pickup.

Then I grabbed my purse and sailed out the door to go to the farmers' market. The fresh air outside focused me and I surveyed the neighborhood in all the layers of history I'd gathered in this place over the years.

I took the route past the empty forested lot around the corner.

Last year someone had discovered a small pack of coyotes there. They were just pups, alone, their mother nowhere to be found. The Neighborhood Patrol called animal protective services and had them removed. Maybe they took them to the Bronx zoo. I looked for them when Aiden and I went there to do some research for a term paper he was writing, and there was a coyote exhibit, but the placard outside their enclosure said simply, *North America*, which meant they could have been anyone's coyotes, not necessarily ours.

On the other side of the street, I saw a homeless man pushing his shopping cart. For years I had watched this man, studied him, as he wandered our neighborhood, wrapped in many layers of clothing. He probably wore everything he owned, so it would never be stolen. His shopping cart was usually full, packed with cardboard for nesting, and plastic bottles that could be exchanged for recycling change. Every now and then, I saw him at the coffee shop stealing a small jug of juice. Sometimes when I was at home, for no apparent reason I would start to think about him, imagine what he was doing at that moment.

Now I followed him on to the commercial strip, the village square, at the edge of our neighborhood. It was a small block, with the coffee shop, a pub, a little grocery, the bus stop, and a plaza with a bench at the center where a statue of a military man towered over it.

The statue wore boots and a uniform, and there was a weapon at his belt. A bronzed plaque dedicating the statue was, due to poor planning, positioned so high on the pedestal that it could not be read without a ladder. But once Jack had hoisted a young Aiden onto his shoulders and asked him what numbers were listed there, since at the time he recognized numbers but could not read words. 1-9-1-8. We decided it was either for those who had fallen during World War I, or it was to commemorate one thousand nine hundred eighteen lives lost in some unknown battle. Either way, this hunk of stone, now so arbitrary to us, must have been the culmination of thoughtful petitions and fundraising and effort. Upon its completion, there might have been a ribbon-cutting ceremony, and all the people in our neighborhood would have come out. Some would have cried.

Now all those imagined people were dead, and the statue was just a place where people hung out after the pub closed. That morning, since it was still early, just one middle-aged couple sat on the bench eating the breakfast that they'd bought at the grocery. She drank coffee; he ate a roll. They were not talking but seemed comfortable. He had an arm slung behind her. At one point, without a word, they switched. She took his roll and he took her coffee. I wondered if Jack and I would ever have circled back to such a comfortable quiet place. Would I even have wanted that?

I hopped the bus for a few stops and then exited at The Quarter. Bypassing its more sprawling parts, I veered directly down one of the bright commercial streets which led to the farmers' market. In search of a proper coffee, I peered into a shop on the corner to look at the menu. There was mocha with homemade vegan marshmallows. The store two doors down made a lovely cappuccino capped by a fading, foamy heart. I stopped at the Bru window to peek in on their weekly tasting. A crowd of people stood around the bar sipping and swirling and tasting and rating the impossible sour green behind the flavor of their beans.

I crossed the street and pushed open the door at Fair Cup. The man tending the counter greeted me, melancholy and soft-spoken, his arms tattooed in a tapestry.

"Coffee whipped with butter and coconut oil," I told him after carefully studying my choices. When he gave me the paper cup, I took a sip and grimaced.

"It's gamey, right?"

"Exactly," I mused. "Strange." But after a moment, I was used to the flavor. "It's actually good." I left the shop and took another long sip. The drink made its way down the core of my body as I walked. By the time I reached the farmers' market, I felt awakened to the possibilities.

Since dawn the market tents had been rising from the pavement, with trucks backed up and unloading fruits and vegetables and dairy products. Each booth boasted something different. Here was charcuterie, and there were homemade candies and jellies. Here was a buttermilk dairy; there a farm bakery serving only pies. During the course of the day, there would be more umbrellas raised, and the crowds would come, carrying burlap sacks or rolling neat little shopping carts—a vibrant center of hipster commerce. But so early in the day, the trucks were the center of action. Their beds opened up to scatter loose hay onto the pavement, their tires smelling of manure pats and country roads.

"What's good today?" I asked my favorite vegetable seller. An old fashioned set of scales at the center measured and tallied each purchase.

"Everything's good," he grinned.

Carrots with clumps of earth still clinging to them and teased out tops in tufts; fat ugly tomatoes that could be eaten like peaches; an anonymous bounty of greens, kale and collards stalked with red and yellow stripes, their dinosaur leaves recalling some primitive rain forest. I bought a few sweet heads of lettuce and a sack of cherries.

Strolling through the stalls that day, for the first time in a long time, the memory of my grandmother's farm in Israel came back to me. There the rhythms of the land offered harmony and purpose to the humans who took their living from it, narrowing body, brain, and soul in a kind of intersecting balance. Sometimes I had been recruited to help with farm work, but mostly I pleasured in it. There, in the height of the plenty, I dug in, a greedy monkey, filling my stomach with bananas and clementines and scattering the peels. I pulled refreshment from the trees or the milk pails or the egg crates, in wordless, unthinking luxury, like a stretch or a sigh.

Looking around at the other shoppers, I imagined that most had never spent time on a farm, like me. Many, I supposed, had never seen more open space than Central Park. But this market drew everyone, linked to some primal memory of good earth that belonged to all people equally.

I had been coming to this market ever since it had opened, but now, with Philip's charge hovering behind me, I started to see the details to which I'd never paid attention. I felt an energy around me that I had never noticed before.

I shouldered my sack as I reached the stand of one of the local dairies. The guys were busy by the truck, so I popped open a small bottle of raw milk. I sipped the milk and watched as two farm-hands with ponytails and tank tops pulled enormous trays of hand-wrapped cheese wedges from the bed. When they were finished, I bought a brick of Parmesan and a tub of soft goat cheese. Then I stopped at the bakery stand for a warm roll spread with fresh butter.

I took a bite and chewed slowly, tasting the salted cream melting into yeast and dough. It reminded me of breathing ocean air, and I felt more whole than I had felt in a long time. When was the last time I had tasted anything like this? Not even while cooking at Channing and fiercely checking off recipe after recipe, and stacking up walls of pickle jars and chutney jars like a fortress around the office. Here, I was newly single-minded, braced with a kind of purpose for all the bounty before me.

Weighed down from my purchases, I lumbered back to the bus stop, and then sat to wait on an empty bench. Slowly, the area began to fill with other people. A young mother nearby paced with her stroller. As she passed me, I peered at the infant. "Just remember, it's all about survival right now," I told her.

"What's that?" she bristled. She hadn't quite heard me, but she seemed to sense the bother of someone older and meddlesome.

"You can't do anything wrong in the early days. All that's important is that everyone lives through it."

The woman gave a tight nod and moved away.

Older women had offered such advice to me when I was a young mother. The baby was too hot. The baby was too cold. Always spoil the baby. Never spoil the baby. At the time, I was fragile and sleep-deprived, feverishly reading all the latest studies on pacifiers and allergies and homemade purees. How to nurse the baby, and how to wean. How to be a helicopter parent, how to not be a helicopter parent. And all those old women had been so certain of themselves that I started to doubt everything.

When Aiden was around two years old, I was swinging him at the park. He was shouting and trying to jump off and flailing his feet. A grandmother playing with her granddaughter nearby turned to me.

"Have you had your boy looked at?" She pursed her lips into a pale bud. "I'd be worried." I only stared at her edgily, jaw clenched. Was she right? She was probably right. She must be right.

That evening, I put him in the tub with Jack's sister's daughter, Lillianna, who was just about the same age. Aiden ate some of the soap and banged his head on the faucet and tried to climb the slippery tiled walls. Meanwhile, Lillianna quietly read her bath books and eventually stood up to shampoo her hair and then Aiden's, too. Yes, I realized, it must be a problem with Aiden in particular. Perched at the edge of the tub, I saw that with certainty now.

"Could it be a boy-girl thing?" Lillianna's mother asked, trying to ease my worries.

"No. Boys and girls are the same until society gets to them." I frowned. "Aren't they?"

Lillianna was nuanced and coordinated, where Aiden was an insatiable physical creature, trying to chew, straddle, poke, and pull everything around him. What in the world was wrong with him? I wondered.

But by the time he was four and a half, he'd started to read and paint. And he would often sit dreamily staring into space. "What's going on in your head?" I would ask him as I cut boiled chicken and carrots for his dinner.

"Things I want to invent," he said once. "A story I'm making up," he told me another time. And I realized that all those old ladies offering advice had never been me, with this child, in these circumstances and these times. Maybe there were helpful grains, but really their wisdom was just nostalgia.

Eventually, I started to want back all those days when I had worried about Aiden, spotting the mistakes and delayed milestones, scheduling his days with all the back to back activities that could fix and groom him, when it was only just the growing that had to happen so he could be exactly who he needed to be. I would have given anything to see the little boy in the tub again, acting like a wild Viking out on the ocean. Even since Jack had left, some days when life was too quiet and Aiden was too busy, I would relive those hours when all he'd wanted was for me to listen to him chat on and on about the powers he imagined in the Lego hunk in his hand.

There never seemed to be enough time for those moments when he was young—or it was there, and I just didn't know how to extract it. Eventually that time was lost, dispersed like a powder puff in the air. Now that I am older, all that time has since been cosmically gathered up—grain by grain, minute by minute—and reapportioned. So these days I have more time than I know what to do with. But it is empty and stretched now as I wait it out in a body full of aches and creaking bones, a thing I don't recognize.

Old women with their advice—even me, too, there at the bus stop, in my forties then but sensing the changes that would someday come—we were just scrambling to reclaim those hours somehow, to pull them back while they could still have meaning. I saw vitality in the faces of young mothers, and envied their round bodies and tangible exhaustion which proved just how much they were needed. So I started to imagine that I, too, had some wisdom.

I settled back on the bus stop bench and soon noticed a figure walking past. Something about his profile seemed familiar. At a distance, I heard the bus rolling forward, heavily. I felt myself drawn to this stranger. When he turned his face toward the bus, I suddenly recognized his blond profile. He happened to glance over his shoulder, then did a double-take and spun around.

My eyes widened: "Sawyer?"

A look of confusion crossed his face. "Do I know you?" He squinted.

"Talia," I helped him. "I subbed for a class you were in years ago. My father was your professor."

Suddenly it dawned on him, and his face broke into a grin. "Are you taking the bus?" he asked as it pulled up in front of us. I boarded first, swiped my card and sat down at the back. He followed and sat down in the seat next to me.

"I never expected to see you again." He shook his head. "What are you doing these days?"

"I'm teaching again. What about you?"

When I'd first met him that semester, Sawyer was a Music Major on a full scholarship, handsome to the point of being pretty with thick blond lashes and a country tan. He'd had a perfectly scrubbed face, still fresh from farm life and honest work. He took his guitar with him wherever he went, and everyone talked about him—students, faculty, too—as a rare talent, almost a musical genius. "He can master any instrument," I'd heard one of his professors say in the faculty lounge. "He can improvise any style. Whatever he does with his talent someday, that boy will be a star."

Sawyer was older than the other students, in his late twenties. He was always clean and neat, but his clothes were modest, each day's outfit almost the same as the one from the day before. The simplicity set him apart in a population of rich, bored, and well-oiled kids doing Ecstasy in the city on the weekends. In those circles, everything was branded, all debates were theoretical, all opinions were somehow equal. So it was exotic the way he was plain, the way his ideas were fiercely real. At first it seemed unusual, but eventually it—and his music— attracted people to him. Girls, especially, were drawn to his charm, in a way that he himself did not see.

Sawyer's writing revealed that he was still that farm boy. He wrote that he missed the fields back home, and that made me miss my own *back home*, and I told him in my red-marker comments in the margins of his papers that his fields must be the long lost cousins of the fields of my grandmother's farm.

Yet, there was darkness within him. Sawyer wrestled in his writing with what it meant to have more than others, to have been plucked out of the cornrows by a scholarship. He wondered about how he might someday use his education, and of course, all the many things he could do with the gift of music. And the straddling nomadic sensibility that tugged at him with the excess of that campus, tugged at me, too, if differently, as I grappled in the same way I always did with the haves and have-nots.

Once, only once, we sat together in the library long after I'd finished giving him feedback on a paper. He had his guitar slung over the back of his chair, as always. And he told me he was worried that home would never feel like home again. We were there until 10:00

o'clock when the library closed. It almost felt as if we were on a date. Had he not been my student, and had I not been married—with Jack at that very moment, home, helplessly patting a bawling Aiden—I would have fallen for him that night.

I only saw Sawyer that one semester. But I remember hearing about him later from my father. And there, on the bus, I felt that same connection dating back from who he was then, and who I was then, me teaching in my father's classroom, bewildered and out of place, so solitary, wearing the kind of bun it *seemed* like a professor should wear and playing the part as best I could.

"And you?"

"I'm a consultant, mostly. And I'm teaching a class as an adjunct, too." He ran a hand through his hair. He looked the same, just with a few gray streaks. "Most of my teaching was done at a college in Oregon, you know, so I'm starting over here. I need to catch up with some of the current research."

"Yes," I slapped the bus seat in front of me. "My father told me you had an article in *Smithsonian*."

He nodded. "And I was going to work at a think tank in D.C.—before it lost funding. I'm all over the place, that's for sure." He laughed.

"So you didn't go home?"

"A few years ago I tried." He looked away for a breath. "But it didn't work out. Now I'm back here for good. After all, this is where the money is." He smiled, and part of me understood that smile, but it also made me sad.

"So I guess that means you're all grown-up now."

"Ah right." He gave me a sly look. "Because I was the student back then, and you were the grown-up professor."

This made me smile. "I was only pretending to be a grown-up then. Still am, as a matter of fact."

We had nothing to say for an awkward moment, and then we each spoke at once, interrupting each other, then stopped, and then laughed, which was often something staged in movies. But, I guess, it really does happen. We had reached a point in the conversation where catching up with an old acquaintance could be politely and pleasantly concluded. But I didn't want that. He might get off the bus at any moment. I watched as he started to gather his bags.

"Listen," I threw out, "would you like to come over for lunch tomorrow?"

He took my address and promised to come at noon.

7.

I set my alarm clock for early the next morning so that I could get in line at Dommy's Bakery. I wanted to see for myself what all the rapture was about with cropiedos.

"I can't believe you're going there," Aiden prodded me the day before when I'd told him my plan. Home from the farmers' market, I'd spent the day writing coupon text in the living room as he wandered in and out and packed to go to Jack's place. "After all your talk..."

Like everyone else in this city, I'd heard about cropiedos for months, and I was curious. But when I learned there was a line out the door for them, I remember telling Aiden, "I'm not going to wait two hours for pastries. Forget the ridiculous name, but anything sold out by 10:00 am is *not* the pastry for ordinary folks like me."

By that morning, the media blitz had switched course. I entered The Quarter, passed the farmers' market, and turned down a road I had never been down before. It was still in the commercial area, but just a bit off the beaten track. The wait turned out to be only an hour. "Because Julie's in Chelsea launched a new kind of grilled ice cream," the woman in front of me said, "people have been sleeping out there in tents all night."

At the counter, I ordered the Rose Petal Rhubarb cropiedo, the Chocolate Mud, and the Lemon Cloud. It wasn't just me, I saw, but everyone there felt compelled to order with kingly grandeur. No one ordered a single pastry. Surely, no person actually needed more than one cropiedo. Each in itself was as big as an elephant's ear, and made up of croissant dough stuffed with a pie filling, donut fried, then rolled and presented in a mason jar made of white-chocolate.

But everyone seemed to want to have the variety, an array of flavors from which to choose. More than a mouthful of anything, it was an experience that people were coming for. But when I finally took a bite, the pastry crackled and dipped at all the right moments, and afterwards, it was hard to believe I had ever doubted them.

Outside, I saw the woman who had been in line with me. Standing at the corner, bent over the box, she tasted her cropiedos. She held each pastry gently, cradling the weight before returning it to its mason jar. She seemed to be searching for words, as everyone believed themselves to be critics, obliged to weigh in importantly: "The lemon maple filling? Perfection!"

"What do you think about that ridiculous wait now?" I asked, taking a last nibble.

"An act of faith," she assured me, her eyes shiny as moons. "The universe is wise—so much wiser than any one person." Carefully, she closed the box and wrapped the string around it in order to save some pastries for later. She gave a half-smile, laughing at herself like she'd learned some important lesson, like she had earned the stickiness.

———

After I got home, I started looking online for recipes to make for lunch with Sawyer. I had some ground lamb, and the sweet lettuce from yesterday. Something Mediterranean? I moved from web site to web site. Making recipes was nothing new to me. Hell, I'd been doing that as a freelancer, I'd been doing that in my campus office. But now that I was determined to see what Philip saw in food, I kept pushing for something bigger.

I clicked on a side link at EatOut, and looked through upcoming events on Food Planet. A photography exhibit called "Bitches of the Block" on female butchers. A review on the new midtown restaurant, Stark.

"On the night of our visit, occasionally, pairings were unbalanced. A butter-cake sea bass, for example, almost disappeared behind a robust cilantro-grapefruit purée and a layer of sweet lime foam. But the tender beef and mint-scented sweet peas in crunchy bird's-nest pastry would have been too rich without the mildly sour pickle mango pink gelée to cut it, and the violet horseradish sorbet provided some much needed heat. All in all, there could have been no greater tribute to the flavors of an Everyman childhood."

A bit bewildered, I clicked on a link to an interview with Stark's head chef, Carlos Venger, trying to uncover the secret behind his heralded Grilled Cheese.

"Well, it came to me a long time ago," he explained in the video, a little misty-eyed. "I tasked myself with creating a Platonic ideal, a 'picture on the cave wall' of Grilled Cheese. My memory of Grilled Cheese, broken down and crystalized at its essence." I hit the pause button.

I wasn't sure what that meant. But if food were not actually so important, would people have the nerve to call some Grilled Cheese a Platonic ideal? You can't go around calling just anything a Platonic ideal. It would mean an utter breakdown. There would be the Platonic ideal of diapers, the Platonic ideal of bowling. Nothing would ever again actually be remarkable. The ripples of this were endless.

Suddenly doubtful, I clicked out of Food Planet and typed in the web address for Recipe Roundtable, a practical place. I decided to make lamb meatballs with a lemon yogurt sauce and salad. I chopped onion, garlic cloves, fresh mint, and cilantro. Then I combined them with parcels of ground lamb, salt, pepper, cumin, coriander, cinnamon, mixing all together in a bowl and forming balls.

It felt good to be in the kitchen. Any doubts, any absurdity, went away with the wholesomeness in my hands. I was lost in the motions of the smallest task, forming perfect globes, all equal in size, not too packed, not too fluffy, with specks of herb dotting the surface like an earth composed only of islands. It was meditative to let everything else fade, abandoned to the repetition of kneading hands. It was leisurely and sensual but it came with that sense of purpose I felt, cooking in the dark at Channing, like art only for the pursuit of art.

While the meatballs baked, I prepared the sauce of yogurt and lemon zest, more cilantro, mint, and cumin. Then I ripped the juicy lettuce leaves, diced cucumbers, tomatoes, onions, squeezed a lemon and drizzled olive oil on top with some kosher salt. Right before we ate I would sprinkle the salad with zaatar and maybe some crumbled flax crackers.

I was scrolling through my playlists when Sawyer came to the door. "Here, you pick." I handed him the iPod and went to the refrigerator. "Beer?" Then I popped my head back out, looking slyly at my former student. "You *are* old enough to drink, aren't you, kid?"

I opened two cold ones, made the final touches to our food, and balancing a tray through the house, took them out to the deck.

"Your Dylan playlist," he smiled following me, as he chose the first song.

"Good choice." I sat down. "The voice of the nation...until he wasn't."

I set out plates and dished up salad and lamb meatballs for us both. "I once read an interview with Dylan, and he was asked something like, 'How did you do it? How were you able to speak for a generation?' I was expecting some wise answer, something deep. But he was as perplexed as anyone. And he said something like he didn't know either, like he was just the channel. And it seemed as if one day in the 1980s, he just woke up and was as amazed by what he had done as the rest of us."

"It takes a lot to know that though, that it's something bigger than you. When it's real and when it's just passing through." Sawyer took a drink of his beer and added some of the yogurt sauce to his plate.

We sat together talking long into the afternoon. When the food and beers were done, I brought out two more beers and some remaining cropiedos and the cherries from the market. I told him about Aiden. He told me about his daughter, Emily, who lived in Florida with her mother, a woman Sawyer had dated casually for a couple months. We spoke more about that semester long ago when I taught him, and about adjunct teaching now, and it was easy conversation.

When you share even a small history with someone, just recalling small details and holding them up for mutual admiration is a meaningful exchange. Remembering them together, or remembering them differently, hashing over old days and resurrecting the promises of that time, building upon one piece with another until something bigger than you expected has suddenly been reconstructed.

"That college was so rich it was shiny," he laughed at one point.

"And so white... They're still talking about me there," I added. He had a way of looking at me when I spoke. And whatever he saw, it pulled me to him, the way I might feel drawn to my own image in the mirror, compelled to stop and straighten and smile into it, transforming for it into my better self.

While we laughed, a new reality settled over us. Years ago, we had both been straddlers. But we had also been at starkly different stages. Suddenly we now found ourselves in quite similar positions, two rootless academics. Single. Masters of some small niche of a niche that could translate into work, but not necessarily, and not reliably. We were, newly, equals.

"Teaching is great. But I don't know how I'd ever earn a living in the system." Sawyer shook his head. "I don't even know what a university will look like in twenty years: everything remote, headless, shapeless, wickedly expensive. Or maybe free."

"At least you still have your music, right?" I reminded him. "Not like this useless purgatory I've made for myself in freelance. What do *I* do when I'm not teaching?" I sniffed. "Today, I proofread coupons for honeydew, and dish soap fifty percent off. Chances are I'll be doing more of the same once the semester is finished."

"What would you do differently, honestly, if you had it to do all over again? Say that you were back twenty years and in college yourself?" He dropped a stripped cherry pit and stem onto his plate.

"I would have done more then, instead of expecting to do more in the future. Time passes and opportunities pass and you wonder how you ever believed there was all that promise in the first place."

"It can't really be that simple."

"It actually might be. When I wrote my play, I was hungry for everything. Love, success, adventure. I always thought it was some complicated arrangement of those *things* that inspired me. But really it was the hunger itself. And," I added after a moment, "having an audience. Anyway, I still write down ideas sometimes—my own stuff I mean, not just grocery specials. Maybe I'll do something with them again someday." I wanted to change the subject. "What about you? Is there anything you would do differently?"

"I don't think so. College was a dream." He dipped his head, like a former high school favorite or football captain recalling his glory days. "Maybe I would have been less of a womanizer that one year."

"*Were* you a womanizer?"

"Not on purpose." He laughed. "Other than that though, what regrets do I have?" He was quiet for a moment.

He went into the kitchen and helped himself to two more beers for us, then sat down again. It seemed like he had made a decision. He drank deeply from his bottle. "Look, I don't regret Emily, not a bit. She's the best thing in my life. But since she was born, and I've turned everything upside down to provide for her, I've changed. You asked if I still make music?" He pointed to his guitar propped up in the corner of my living room, visible where we sat outside. "I do. But almost never for myself."

"So, for whom then?"

"For anyone who will pay me."

"I'm sure it's not that bad." I laughed it off. "You're not the first parent—or the last—to do what has to be done to put food on the table."

"It *is* that bad," he confessed suddenly, with the relief and certainty of someone who has lived too long with a truth. "I've been part of some awful things. Made music for messages so repulsive they need to hide behind the notes. Propaganda, corporations, foreign governments, interrogations. You name it. Persuasion beyond the pale—turns out that's my biggest talent."

I scoffed. But he was quiet, waiting for me to believe the full extent of his confession, and how far he had fallen from where he was years ago, when once everyone had spoken of his genius and potential. "I'm sure you're exaggerating," I postured. Silently, I searched the torn look on his face, and after a moment, though I could not read what haunted him, I could almost hear it: the hypnotic music he'd made to recruit soldiers, the maddening music he'd made to torture captives, the con-man music he'd made to sell, sell, sell. And with all the angst over the things he'd done, there was even more, his own crushing loss of what he could have been. I had felt this too at times, but his defeat seemed even deeper somehow, and was lodged in a more fixed, hopeless place.

"Say something," he said miserably after it had been quiet unbearably long.

I went to him and put my arms around him. At first it was awkward, if only because it seemed to acknowledge what he'd said. His shoulders slumped and he let out a weary sigh. But when I felt the thumping inside his chest, something happened to me. It was like I woke up all at once, the way I always wanted to. Maybe it was just the strange sensuality of suddenly being so close to another human being. Breathing the warmth of Sawyer's shirt and chest, I suddenly felt a potential I hadn't felt in years, to fix the unfixable, to attain the unattainable. I felt a trembling urgency. What had deadened him, seemed to awaken me.

Sawyer left towards evening. But we promised we would see each other again in a few weeks when he returned from Florida after Thanksgiving. Meanwhile, I closed the door softly behind him and walked to my desk. I sat down slowly, uncertainly, not quite sure what to do with my new restlessness, my re-invigorated sense of being awake and energized in the world. I moved aside my freelance notes, pushed away the copy for grocery coupons in the next issue. Instead, I dug out Penny's large manila folder and started to sift through her poems again.

Sometimes, when I was tinkering with my freelance work, I'd look up at the picture of JB Picard above my desk. I'd put him up there hoping for inspiration for the magnificent play I'd hoped to write but never had written. But even when I faltered with researching carrots or baking soda hacks and new ways to write coupons, I would picture JB Picard at his writing instead, fifty epic novels, each with a unique and intricate world that spanned a thousand pages. Everything else, certainly my coupons, always seemed easier in comparison. I'd try to imagine the way JB Picard's brain could create a sympathetic sadist, or define a whole fictional code of chivalry so intricately that when it was broken it felt shocking and barbarous, as if that code had actually been real. The dizziness that came from picturing him at work was one of the only things that allowed me to piece together a tapestry of grocery tidbits and five-step recipes. Now, as I began reading through Penny's pages, JB Picard again looked over me, and her pages began to pass in a flurry of light and clicks and purpose.

In the morning, I pulled out Jack's coffee grinder and French Press and tried to make coffee for myself, like the one from the day before, whipped with coconut oil and butter. The first one was okay but too greasy, so I tried again, with less butter and more coconut oil. But that one was too thin. When I finally got it right on my sixth try, I took it with some biscotti to the television. I placed the mug and plate on coasters and then moved through the living room pulling down blinds. I settled in on the couch and turned the television to Food Show.

It had been a long time since I'd watched anything on the network, and now I was tuned in to the end of a classic black and white Margo Sesame show. Her old-fashioned trill voice and crisp white apron lightened the room with optimism, the sense that all was right, or could possibly be made right. I sank deeply into the cushions, enjoying the coffee, the biscotti, seeing Margo Sesame float through the studio kitchen, tying a roast with twine, waxing poetic over scrubbed potatoes. It made me feel whole.

Following Margo was a baking competition, in which the judges crowned a winner—first laughing over her punchy, whimsical layers of merengue and lavender cream, then weeping over the bittersweet nostalgia in her deconstructed chocolate torte.

Next was an episode of the *Cut* competition. It was an ordinary cooking contest, up until the end, when they declared a winner, and the loser could choose an escape hatch—some dare or feat that, if accomplished, would let them leap-frog to victory and the prize money. That day for the escape hatch, the host and loser walked into a butcher shop set with a glass case full of whole, plucked raw chickens.

"We call this The Wishbone Pick." The host offered a small, neat smile. "To start, you pick your bird."

The loser surveyed his choices and finally pointed to a pale, goose-bumped hen in the corner, her plump drumsticks crossed rather daintily over a bed of leafy green. Then he was escorted to a table and the hen placed upon a plate before him.

"Your challenge is to find the wishbone and leave it intact but sparkling clean. In less than three minutes. You'll notice," the host pointed out, "no silverware. No tools permitted, other than the ones nature gave you."

The loser was rather stunned. But as soon as the timer started, he sprang into action. He picked up the chicken, and with bare hands started pulling it apart, slimy skin slipping, bones cracking, pink flesh tearing as he searched for the space where the wishbone lay buried. The audience, seated closely around the stage, cheered him on, but I could not believe my eyes and grew more and more appalled as he tore into the dead raw animal with ever greater ferocity. Why would anyone agree to this humiliation, this grotesque torture, for some televised food competition? The horror of the dismemberment in miniature spread over me.

In less than a minute the loser had found the wishbone but now he had to carefully pull it clear from the flesh. Once he had done all he could with his hands, he started sawing away the gristly parts with his teeth. The terrible mouthfuls seemed to clear any remaining hesitation from him. Grimacing now, he chewed off large morsels of the cold flesh, spitting out a bone to discard every now and then, undoubtedly swallowing some of the meat as he went. With just a minute left, he moved on to the more delicate gnawing of the smaller bits to render it clean.

I sat watching in horror, but to my dismay the audience was enthralled, shrieking and chanting, *wishbone, wishbone, wishbone!* Someone ran up from the back of the auditorium to collect a portion of the chicken carcass as a souvenir. What was wrong with them? Then, suddenly, I was struck by an unexpected flash of understanding. I cocked my head and moved closer to the television. Was that all there was to it? I looked at the loser, eating; I looked at the audience again. What was that expression on their faces?

In fact, *this* was what Philip had been referring to all along. There was something vital in this eating, something that the loser understood; something that the audience screamed for, something that brought everyone to this spectacle and held their attention to the very end.

I sat on the carpet right in front of the television for the final seconds. I watched each close-up of the skin and meat and fat, the broken bones, the controlled way in which the loser held back a heave, then steadied himself, then ploughed onward with a kind of admirable grit. At last, with only seconds left, he triumphantly held up the shiny clean wishbone. As the loser—now winner—did a victory lap around the butcher shop set before quietly throwing up in the corner, I leaned back, amazed. "What the hell?" I asked the television. But no, oh yes, I finally understood!

That ghastly eating was actually a magnificent bending of will and nature. Food was power. And all those mothers I had seen over the years who fed their children protectively, compulsively, knew it. Bottles of milk, scrapings of porridge, sandwiches cut into triangles. *Have more meat. Are you hungry? Do you need more? Eat! Eat!* Food was a force. And everyone knew it.

But food could also be transcendence. A competitor's determination, rising above both circumstance and his gut with sheer will power: that was art. It was almost beautiful. I leaned my back against the coffee table.

This world of food, and its true magnificence, was so much more than laboring over recipes, or even the pleasure of farm and table. It was defying nature and instinct and the gravity of the mundane, drawing upon hidden wells of creativity to take the same pot and the same bread from thousands of years ago, and not merely eat from habit, but reinvent it into infinity.

I shook my head, excited. If only I could truly grasp it, then I would be alive again. Hell, anyone would be, even someone like Sawyer! If only he could see this too, this shrugging off of ancient human experience for the new and brilliant, then he would be saved from the dark places his music had taken him. And somehow it would circle back to me again, and save me too. Because there was a link there, an electrical circuit between us: If I could wash everything away for him, the need, the haunting defeat, then it would somehow wash away everything from me as well. Everything I'd wanted some wise man in India to tell me would come from this instead.

The next show was a re-run of the annual parade featuring food trucks from all over the country. There was a truck from Chicago pulling a mermaid float with the chefs handing out their caviar and vodka popsicles. Then a truck came from Austin with honest-to-goodness rattlesnake custard. There was a truck that seemed to be devoted to nothing but kimchi pies, then a couple of retro food trucks. More and more trucks passed. Some passed out free samples. One of the shawarma trucks had a stage with a belly dancer atop. And then the boutique truck that usually parked near 5th Avenue, a tall truck with all-glass sides and hundreds of tiny boxes tied in whimsical ribbon lining the shelves inside it. "It's like getting a birthday present. You don't even choose, and you don't know what you get until after it's yours," the show host explained, untying the ribbon of the box he had been given. "It could be anything: dice-sized cubes of fudge, thin curly strips of wild cherry deer jerky, perfect little globes of bright agar, miniature Macadamia-nut cookies. Or this…" He pulled an exquisite red glass bottle from his box. "Strawberry vinegar!" He downed it in one shot.

I went into the kitchen during a commercial and made myself another cup of coffee and brought it back to the sofa. I watched *Cooking Caveman* and *Saving Face* with Ronny Dutch. Each show I studied earnestly now, trying to inhale the details, listening for what might resonate. Then my phone rang. "What are you doing?" Philip asked.

"Watching *The Adventures of Lena Potts*," I told him, walking to my desk. "And all these other shows. It's pretty marvelous."

"Isn't it? You sound giddy."

"Also, there's this guy…"

"Ah," he interrupted, "I told you that you needed to get laid."

"What? No, it's not like that."

"Well," he pouted, "it should be. No matter. I used to have a thing with her brother. Did I ever tell you that?"

"Who?"

"Lena Potts. She's kind of a sage in the food world. Margo Sesame's niece, you know. She was a prodigy from the start, and now with all of Prongs' success… We're all still friends," he added. "She wasn't on site the other night when we were at Purr. And I'm too busy to take you myself anytime soon. But maybe I can get you in to Prongs. If you want, I can arrange for you to meet her."

And that was how I first came to Prongs.

8.

Prongs was in The Quarter right around the corner from the farmers' market. It was a numberless address at an understated warehouse door that I'd previously not noticed. That evening, after they'd double-checked me on the list, I was led past the train station and past Purr where Philip and I had eaten. I found myself inside an unexpected glass tunnel, which led to a sleek underground bar. There, I immediately picked out Lena.

She wore a tangerine baby-doll dress, wedge shoes, a stark bob with bangs and bright red lipstick. She gave orders to the wait-staff. She tasted a wine before shaking her head disapprovingly and summoning another bottle as a replacement. She greeted a known patron as she floated past me at the bar, casually flipping her hair with overflowing confidence. Even in my most poised moments, I had never come close to such a self-possession and charm. I could see at once why Philip loved her. And I could see why he wanted us to meet. She was the incarnation of food—at least the new generation of it, and well, maybe of everything.

"Shall we do it?" she asked, sitting down on the stool across from me, draping an arm over the bar and crossing her legs in the other direction in one seamless movement.

Lena smiled like an old-fashioned movie starlet, though she was obviously uncomfortable with sentimentality. She was at ease with her body in a way that women of my generation had to talk themselves into—a fluidity that came so naturally to her generation as they used their bodies to starve, cut, dye, document, give pleasure, take pleasure, and own. Lena drank everything from a wine glass.

"It's the perfect vehicle. It's art." She flourished her glass at me. "Why should we settle for anything less?" As the bartender approached, Lena asked me, "What are you drinking tonight?"

"Vodka cranberry," I almost apologized.

She sized me up quickly, sniffing the air like a mariner might while directing the bartender to *add a twist of lime, a sprig of mint, a ring of sea salt.* She turned back to me. "Don't worry, it will be perfect." And she was right. Maybe Philip would have said it was dead-on instincts and a nose for the next trend, but as I saw it, she had, in all things to do with appetite, a kind of clairvoyance.

"Lena is driven," Philip had told me on the phone when we'd first spoken of her. "She's in another dimension, with another calling. We're all just dinosaurs compared to her."

"Philip told me that you are new to food, and curious." She licked her lips. "Any pet of Philip's is a pet of mine. So what can I tell you?"

I faltered for a second, suddenly not sure what exactly there was to know or why I was there. "How did all this happen?"

She didn't pause. "In my case, it was a bit unusual, and fast. I didn't rely on my Sesame family connections. I wanted to do my own thing. Once Pepper Pops became a franchise, I got a lot of interest from Food Show and other entrepreneurs." She listed some of her upcoming projects, including another Food Show pilot. "Why say no? Everything is a creative opportunity." This was the key to her genius: if her instinct said yes, the ordinary inhibitions, the checks and balances, just didn't exist for her. And her relationship with everything was uncommon, not just food. Fame, too. She seemed not to notice patrons in the bar gawking at her. And she dismissed a recent breakup with some big-shot Hollywood actor, Sky Walter, flipping her hair and waving it off with one hand.

"There have been some great gigs," she continued, "but they were all just leading up to me getting the financing to buy this space and build Prongs. Philip still talks about collaborating someday. He wants us to do a film together maybe, but this place is what I was waiting for, really. It's always been my dream. It's what I was born to do." She gestured around the room, not overly dramatic but fiercely certain.

"This is a place where any food vision can come to life." She hopped off her stool. "Let me show you around; not everything, of course, just a few rooms. You'll come back another time for a proper experience."

I followed her out of the bar and down a grand set of stairs that descended even further underground. We emerged in a long passageway, like an ancient cavern, with spans of scrubbed concrete and polished industrial piping, so the whole space appeared glassy. Fat lights that looked like torches were mounted on the ceiling. The air felt cool and smelled of incense. Harp music played at low volume from speakers hidden in pockets of stone.

"We start with the kitchen, of course." She stopped at a door. Like all the doors within the hallway, it was a sheet of silver chains. Lena punched a code into a small keypad. Suddenly the chains parted and she ushered me inside a bright kitchen. Or was it a laboratory?

A landscape of fiery ranges and sterile counters, knives so sharp and thin they looked transparent, modern gadgets hanging overhead, food processors and blowtorches and test tubes that combined the cells of two different foods on a molecular level, and machinery that could print meatballs in 3D, as well as many more gadgets made of sleek stainless steel that I didn't recognize. But also, there were entire shelves filled with antique mortars and pestles and teakettles and clay ovens and smokers and sharp grates poking up like ribs. We walked through the smaller kitchenettes meant for specialty preparations, and the refrigerator, the freezer, the pantry; all stocked with every imaginable fruit, vegetable, grain, seed, nut, meat, fish, poultry, milk, nectar, oil, vinegar, cheese, and spice.

"Daniel is a Michelin star chef and owner of two top-ranked restaurants in Paris. But he has specialists working under him, too." Lena pointed proudly to where he worked, guiding a sous-chef in some particular preparation. "What are you working on?" she asked him.

His face lit up. "In the main dining hall, they are having the annual dinner for a Francophile club from upstate. These people are purists, down to the butter and the herbs. Nothing they eat can be made without using traditional French methods. Their secretary, who booked the dinner months ago, warned me that they would taste even the slightest variation in preparation, and after meeting them, I believe her." He triumphantly held up a linen bag. "Won't they be amazed? A harvest of truffles from a forest just outside Paris, meticulously groomed every year going back eight hundred years. Exquisite!"

"Many of our clients come so Daniel can cook for them," Lena told me after he disappeared into the freezer. "But we also have many who come to learn from him. That's big now in The Quarter, and the night market, too, this fascination with Makers. Yesterday he was teaching some sort of Swedish cuisine. And next week he has a party interested in learning how to prepare poisonous fish."

We left the kitchen and went back into the main corridor. I followed her to one of the many anonymous doorways. "This is one of my favorite spaces," she said.

The room we entered was a forest, with thick, leafy trees all around us, and the smell of wet leaves and mossy growth on each breath. Bird calls made it feel like we were outside, but I knew we were still far underground. "Sometimes I come here for my morning yoga," she told me.

"What is this place?" I asked.

She gestured for me to follow her through the woods. "One thing people want, whether they know it or not, is to experience the source of their food. You see it in trends; buy and eat local, and city gardens. But really, it's more primal than that. What people actually want is to hunt."

I looked around more cautiously. "Why don't they just go hunting in a real forest?"

"Well, most people don't want to admit that they hunt, at least not those who live in urban societies. So it's safer here. And the results are certain." We stopped in a small clearing. "Plus, here we can stock the forest with any quarry. No hunter has to go all the way to Africa. And he won't have to worry about customs or the politics of hunting and killing an endangered species." We stopped above the clearing, but still underneath the forest cover. "This month we have cats." There were several cheetahs stretched out on the grass. "We can get anything, even reptiles or elephants, though honestly, they are such a logistical nightmare. And dealing with primates is just bizarre."

"Primates?" I pictured the warm eyes of a gorilla, so full of intelligence and personality. "People really want to hunt and eat primates?"

"No telling what people want." Lena pushed further through the brush.

I followed her, looking every which way through the greenery to see what other creatures might be in hiding in this place that felt to every sense like a real forest. "This is staggering," I gaped.

Her eyes boiled a bit. "It really is, isn't it?"

"How did you even envision something like this?"

"Listen, I'm not the first. People have been adventuring in food for years. There is no end to exclusive daredevil clubs and themed restaurants. Hell, you can go on any given night to The Quarter and stumble upon something ten times wilder than what we have here. But at Prongs, it's refined and curated, perfectly controlled to the exact degree, exactly what people want when they want it—assuming they can pay for it." She led me back through the trees toward the door. "We cater to any fantasy."

She opened the door and ushered me back into the cavern. As we walked she gestured at different rooms. "Different countries, of course. The striptease," she pointed at a door as we passed, "the experience of perfectly synchronized musical notes with flavors." She pointed at yet another door: "Even the food fights and slapstick nonsense." Lena punched in a code and started to open the silver chains of another door, but at that moment something splatted against it from the inside. Turning up her collar, she spoke crisply into a small microphone pinned onto her shirt: "Custard cleanup in forty-three, please."

"Everything joyous and playful; and messy, too," she snorted. "But honestly, I'm interested in more complicated fantasies—those that people don't always want to admit to, or are not only pleasurable, but may involve pain." Lena put an arm around my shoulder. "You might think it's odd, but there is a necessary degree of tragedy in all this, too."

We stopped in front of a door to the right. A small placard on it read: *There are people in the world so hungry, that God cannot appear to them except in the form of bread.* "This is the fasting hall." Lena pointed to the art on the door, showing scenes of meditation and sin and inquisition and the tortures of hell. She cracked the door open for me and we took a step in. The floors were parched mud and sand with only two spots of vegetation visible. The limits of the room faded away because instead of walls or ceilings, sprawling screens showed vast desert and a bleached sky, appearing perfectly real. The unrelenting sun moved across the arc of the dome as the hours of the manufactured day passed. The air was like a dry sauna, smelling of sweet cedar wood. The only sound was the ghostly wind that whipped up sand then subsided. I thought I heard the sound of trickling water nearby, but how could that be?

Lena pointed to a tree at the center of the space. "That fig tree is the only shade." A lone man in some sort of trance sat beneath it. "Usually they come with religious fervor. It lasts maybe a day. This guy's been here for two days now. He took vacation from work for this," she whispered. "This hall is not about food, obviously, though he can collect manna, and he can drink from the spring beneath the castor oil plant." She pointed to a low plant growing to one side, and indeed there seemed to be a thin, stream of water moving beside it, and simple white sponge cakes in a basket. She closed the door and led me back through the hall. "Any longer than three days, I would draw the line. I don't want any more incidents. If someone has a death wish, they need not play it out here," she added tidily.

"What does a guy like that do all day?" I wondered, as we walked by other doors. "Meditate?"

"Some of the time, I guess. We mix a little of this or that into the incense, or into the manna itself, so he's probably out of it much of the time. The clients who come to that room specifically already have something playing out inside themselves, something dark and preoccupying. They don't really need the kind of entertaining that we offer in the other rooms."

"That's pretty crazy."

She agreed matter-of-factly. "But sometimes I feel like what happens in here is so much more real and makes so much more sense than half of what happens outside." She cracked open another door for me to look inside. "This isn't for patrons. This is Jill's lab."

A sullen woman with blue hair mixed some solution over burners, directing a small team of other scientists. The walls of the room were lined with shelves, and the shelves were crammed with bottles of chemicals, pills, herbs, and powders.

"Here's the thing about getting to what's real," Lena explained. "Sometimes you need a bit of help along the way. Something to relax you. Something to stimulate you. Something to entice you, or heighten you from moment to moment." She closed the door as we left. I could see on her face as she spoke the pleasure and relief of a magician finally free to explain a trick. "Jill is a genius. A doctor, a scientist, and an astounding pastry chef, too."

Lena led me further down the hallway and unbolted only the metal over a small glass window in the silver paneling of another door. "I don't want to go inside, but even from here, you can get a glimpse of our fountain of youth."

I peered through the glass and saw a landscape of tropical grass, shade trees, and at the center a bubbling, milky hot spring draped with a curtain of ivy. Several old people, naked forms, moved around inside the room. Some bathed, others leaned against the trees. The truly fragile were being lowered by their aid-workers into the water—dark, beefy men that at one point in life they would never have noticed but were now their best friends. All the older people seemed to be drinking from gourds, their limbs artificially youthful. I looked away, embarrassed to spy on them at their unnatural play.

"Don't worry," Lena assured me, "they can't see you."

I cocked an eyebrow, but she nodded again and I couldn't resist. Pressing my face to the glass again, I tried to see the far off corners of the room, and to smell the heavy flowering bushes of honeysuckle that edged the space. I imagined this is what heaven would be, if heaven somehow existed in a chamber underground.

Suddenly something banged on the other side of the glass. A pale wrinkled face pressed flat to mine from the other side of the window. I pulled back. The woman had short white hair and a spindly neck that led to frail naked shoulders. She somehow seemed to be able to see me, her eyes glazed thick from cataracts, but appearing to look directly into my eyes from behind the glass, blithe but also trapped in her blitheness.

I moved a few paces down the hall. "Are you sure they can't see out?"

"Of course I'm sure." Lena bolted the screen back over the window and led me down another corridor. We stopped at the last door of the hallway. "This is one of Philip's favorite rooms." Lena punched in the key code. "He helped me work out the execution."

When I saw it, I had to smile. "Of course he did."

The hall of slaves smelled like dust and sweat. It radiated in heavy desert heat, and the room itself seemed scorched by endless sunlight. Or was it some other kind of illumination? A man walked past, barefoot, coated in dust, carrying a heavy stone strapped in leather thongs across his back. Nearby several women in rags that barely covered their nakedness held baskets of food, encircled within their arms. They, too, were covered in dust as they made their way to serve a table of patrons who were shaded at the far end of the room.

"For most people, being waited upon at table feels luxurious and intimate. Of course we have many variations on that here. But there are those that also want servitude in its most naked form." She shrugged. "For them, if there's no objectification, then it's somehow lacking."

Another man walked past. The back of his robe was shredded and bloody. I grimaced. "Even to the point of appearing whipped?"

"Not just appearing." She closed the door and led me back down the main corridor. "For all this to work, elements of reality must be woven throughout. The fewer cracks, the tighter each one of these worlds will seem."

"So what are you saying?" I was taken aback.

"Oh we touch things up of course. But we also hand-select the people here. Submissive types. Those who naturally like to dominate. You put them here together in this space with the heat and the expectation, and eventually," she waved her hands, as though she were casting a spell, "they all make their own truths."

Lena led me back to the stairway returning to the Prongs bar. I followed her reluctantly. "Is it greedy of me that I want to see what's inside every room?"

"A bit." She smiled charmingly. "It's actually been fun to see this place anew with you. How lucky that Philip discovered you. And, of course," her eyes narrowed, suddenly cool, "I know Philip would never send me someone who would give away our secrets here." She waited for a response.

"No." I gasped. "I would never say anything!"

"Of course not. That would be unwise. Not to mention, you would never enter this place again." She paused for a moment and then her voice lightened once more. "I really do want you to come back soon. I'm sorry, but I have to run now. It's going to be a full house tonight."

9.

Thanksgiving came and went and all around was pumpkin-flavored nostalgia. But just as quickly, the students returned and began to speak dreamily of the semester break, of Christmas, of Daytona Beach and Jell-O shots and tan lines. Philip and I sat overlooking the quad, drinking a rose tea I had brewed, talking about Penny's senior project, and about Sawyer, who had texted me from Florida several times and was now home. On the shelf above us sat a bottle of rose liquor I was making, and a couple of jars of spicy rose chutney. "Stop deliberating," Philip urged. "If Lena invited you and says there's room for one more, just ask him."

I hesitated and then made a quick decision. *Come out with me tonight*, I texted Sawyer.

Yes. He texted back a few minutes later. *Where?*

Prongs.

"Look at this!" I showed Philip my phone and beaming. "He's in."

He glanced at it and scoffed. "You seem awfully pleased for someone who claims just-friends-no-funny-business."

I disappeared into the kitchen to check the oven, where a rose-infused sponge cake was nearly done baking. When I returned, Philip was gazing through the window where students milled below us, rapt as always, as he studied real life. I neared him to see what he was watching—a group of students wrestling outside like cubs—and snickered. "College is really just the next stage of childhood, isn't it?"

"There's something to that," he agreed. "Everyone shows up. Everyone wins a trophy."

"I've been seeing it here and there all semester. And not just with

95

Penny, either," I shrugged. "I hate to say it, but it's probably a good thing I teach creative writing. I teach craft. I give opinions. I dissect words and connotations. I tell students that there's too much about the mother character or too little about the mother character, or that the sex is trite."

"So the nuance is the point."

"Right. I could never teach a class where I'm delivering singular truths." I nodded. "Who am I to do that?"

"Well, you *are*, we've been told, the Progressive's dream-girl."

"Very funny." I shrugged. Progress—which after my play had seemed to be my calling—now felt that much more bewildering in this academic setting. Here, the compass could quiver with certainty in any direction. "Anyhow, I don't even know what counts as progress or truth here. All your politically correct, blanket progressiveness seems damn near fascist to me."

"Well, some dogmas *are* better than others." He gave a sly smile.

"Seriously. The other day, I ran into Ruth in the copy room. 'Flyers for the student center,' she said, waving her papers. 'They need to know the truth about this war.'

"'You mean what's happening on the ground?' I asked.

"She looked at me stonily. 'I mean, about what our government is doing. About how it's wrong.' She knew with absolute certainty that I had to agree with her, that all educated people agreed with her, and that was truth."

"And it's not? "Philip asked.

I threw up my hands. "It almost doesn't make a difference. It was more that as broadminded as her ideas are, she couldn't see the reality in something like war. I don't mean an indisputable evil or scientific truth. I mean war, which is terrible, true, but it's sometimes unavoidable and sometimes necessary. And if an intelligent, well-intentioned person, a professional educator, can hold that an idea, removed from its reality, is the singular truth, and to even question that is offensive, well, it means those truths that actually *are* indisputable have no safe haven at all." I heaved a great sigh.

"Lord, you're exhausting when you're in your head." Philip nodded for a few moments though, considering my words. Then he brightened. "Even if you're right, the good news is, it's not our problem."

I stayed quiet then, but deep down I felt weak for remaining silent and playing along. As the semester passed, I'd found myself moving through classes and meetings and conferences in a daze. I still remembered some calling from my play, some charge to change the world. So when I started teaching, I half-thought that this was my chance, finally, to make a real difference. But now mid-term, I was certainly not changing the world. Worse yet, I was slowly melting into its machinery.

Getting ready to meet Sawyer that night, I told myself that I was only going to spend time with an old friend; this was *not* a date. But I tried on several outfits in my closet, peeled them off, red-faced and hair-mussed, and then piled them messily upon the bed. And I became irritated at what this fussiness must mean about my real intentions—and more and more determined to protect myself from disappointment. Then I came across my go-to blue dress. When I'd worn it at Philip's party, Ruth told me she liked it, which made me vaguely dislike it. Her only other fashion advice until then had been to point darkly to my oversized Jackie O sunglasses—which I'd congratulated myself on buying during some rare, fashion impulse—and she informed me, "They're only trendy because they make a woman into a faceless stack of body parts. Though, of course," she'd shrugged, "your choice."

Now, anxious to end the deliberation, I took out the blue dress anyway and slammed the closet door shut. I pulled on its cool, known line and drape and, finally, stood comfortably before the mirror. It had a deep V-neck and ruching across the hips. From one side it was form fitting, but from the other side it was somewhat maternal. Still, it showed my calves well, coming just over what I used to call—before I got them myself—middle-aged lady knees. I put on blush and lip-gloss then smoothed my hair. Pretty, if a little washed-up with a slightly slacker jawline than I'd once had. But I felt more awake than I had in years.

We went first for a drink a few blocks from Prongs, at a place that Sawyer recommended. "I used to play here back in the day." It was a delightful little moonshine bar, where they actually had someone at a still making moonshine along the back wall where the band was setting up. I ordered an apple pie moonshine at the bar and Sawyer got a thick tumbler of the sweet-corn kind. We took our drinks to the back and nestled at a small table.

"I wanted to thank you for that night when I last saw you," he said. "I haven't really talked to anyone about what my music has come to. I mean, I almost never let myself think about it." He took my hand across the table. "Well, that's not true. It's in the back of my mind all the time. But for me it was an absolution, and you didn't throw me out." He leaned in and kissed me, just barely touching my lips. He tasted like moonshine, and I fell into it, relieved to not have to pretend I did not want him. When we broke away, he smiled softly. "It was more than that, of course. I can talk to you. And you can talk to me, too." He cocked his head to study me. "So, what about you; what are your terrible confessions, your failures?" He plucked at random. "Tell me what went bad with your marriage."

"It never really went bad. But it had always loomed in the background, what was destined to happen to our relationship. The truth just became obvious. A million small details and off scents from over the years came together." I paused a moment to breathe and consider. "The day we decided to go through with the divorce, we were quibbling over new dining room furniture."

"You're joking, right? You divorced over furniture?"

"It was never about the furniture. We argued about almost everything. Eventually, it became a constant power struggle. I stopped liking him. Then I stopped loving him. And believe it or not, now that it's all over, I've started liking him again."

"Was he controlling?" Sawyer squinted. "Was that it?"

I took a deep breath and spoke in a great rush. "Truth is, I probably never should have married. I'm the last person who should be in a commitment like that. Marriage, even in the best circumstance, is *eat or be eaten*. You do terrible things to each other, things you would never do to a stranger. You dismantle the fantasy one nail at a time. You fight over shitty diapers. You tell yourself lies. You tell each other lies. You show each other the weakest and worst parts of yourself." I stopped and shook my head. "I was just never cut out for it."

"That's more insight than most people get in a lifetime."

"Or want." I laughed.

"You still have a way with words," he mused.

"Ranting, maybe," I smirked.

He shrugged. "You definitely had moments of brilliance in the classroom. You do well telling stories. I bet your play was great."

I frowned. "I've grown to hate-love plays and books. In my next life, I think I won't want to write anymore. I probably won't even read."

"That makes perfect sense," he agreed dryly. In solidarity he offered, "So, I won't either." We finished our drinks listening to bluegrass.

As Sawyer looked at the bill and put money on the table, the band took a break and I excused myself to go to the restroom. When I came out Sawyer was no longer at our table but at the stage at the back of the room. The stage was made to look like a living room painted deep red with a couch and two chairs surrounding a coffee table. Sawyer was sitting on the couch, holding a guitar and talking to one of the band members. The man moved the mike towards him and Sawyer put on a pair of sunglasses he'd pulled from his jacket, as if he didn't want to be recognized. It looked as though they were just sitting around at someone's house. Then they started to play.

First it was raw guitar, so pure it seemed like the strings themselves were just breathing. Then Sawyer began to sing, and his voice descended into some rich folkie baritone. *Let's get away in our heads, let's go off and hide.* His body relaxed, rocking in a kind of rhythmic ownership, feeling the sounds he'd invented and moving into them with a true physical command. I closed my eyes, and everything else went away. *We'll pretend that we're together and play we're drinking wine.* The music could do what nothing else could, so I let it fill me. Indeed, the entire room hushed and watched him, rapt until the song circled around and the guitar faded out. Then the room burst into applause.

After the song, Sawyer joined me at the door. People watched him leave, clearing a space as we moved through the crowd. Almost awkwardly, he said, "Sorry, I couldn't resist. For old times' sake, you know."

"Not bad," I took his hand.

"Thanks." He shrugged. "No matter what the critics tell you about a song, you only really hear what it's about when you're strumming it on a guitar, alone in your room."

I looked at him out of the corner of my eye. "So, what's with the sunglasses?"

He pulled them off his face and tucked one stick underneath the collar of his shirt. "You don't like rock star sunglasses? I know, so cliché, right?" Fidgeting, he pushed them up and into his hair.

I snorted. "A little bit."

He put them back over his eyes, to be contrary. As we walked into the early evening light, the music of the house band faded into a comfortable quiet. "Here's the real question," he said in a low voice. "With or without the sunglasses, do you like me enough to take me home tonight?"

I looked at him plainly. "I don't know yet."

"I think you do," he informed me. "You know in the first minute or two if you want to be with someone."

"Wisdom from your player days, eh?" I thought about what he said. "Anyhow if that's true, what are *you* doing the rest of the time? Just trying not to screw it up?"

"Clever girl." He smiled. "But yes. Back when I still had it."

I felt the moonshine, still warming me. I remembered him years ago, an enviable posture in his bearing, purely present; not expectant but simply charmed and open and free of pretense. "I think you've still got it," I told him softly.

"These days I've lost it." He shrugged. "All of it."

"Not a few minutes ago when you were singing in that bar."

"I can call it up if I try, but it's not real—not like it once was."

"So, what happened?"

"After college, I went back to Ohio. But it was never going to be home there again, so I fled out west, then down south. I fixed up a small sailboat, and sometimes I'd be alone on the ocean off Florida for months at a time."

"Being alone made you feel whole again?"

"When you're alone on the water, the only thing that's real is the water itself. One trip, right before Emily was born, I'd been out on my own for weeks. Maybe I'd lost track of time. I probably could have gone on sailing for decades. Then one day there was a storm. I'd not seen one like that before or since. And I had to jump into the stormy sea to cut the line. It was thousands of feet deep and the fish were three times my size. And there was no one in the boat to pull me back on board." He paused. "After that, you know: everything is just a construct." Then he smiled in a self-deprecating way. "Well, until you settle in and forget it again, anyway."

In our talk, faces close, breath warm, we were making our own little space now, just down the street from Prongs, and everything else faded away.

"Yes," I said suddenly.

"Yes what?"

"Yes, I'm taking you home with me tonight."

He took my arm. "Good. But first I want to see Prongs."

10.

"There's a hiccup with one of the mermaids," Lena told Sawyer and me, rushing around. Then she turned us over to her right-hand man, Peter. "These are my special guests," she told him. "Answer their questions and help them out with anything they want."

"What exactly is the 'hall of royals'?" Sawyer asked, looking around curiously as Peter led us down the stairs.

"The real answer?" Peter raised an eyebrow.

"Of course." I spoke for us both.

"Some of our high-end patrons, sultans and princes, need to bring along their entire kitchen staff, their harems, and their entertainment when they travel. But, if they come to Prongs," he gave a flourish, "they can leave all that at home." We stopped in front of a door. "More commonly, of course, it's for our regular patrons who want to *feel* like those others." He opened the door and ushered us inside.

Thousands of lanterns hung across the cathedral-like ceiling of the hall. They cast a lemon glow above the many tables set with candelabras and goblets, heavy silver. Peter led us to a velvet couch alongside one of the tables—private enough so that we could sink into it and feel intimate if we wanted to, but also placed so that we could lean over and talk to people nearby. It was a mixed group, a set of men who seemed to be on a business trip, an odd collection of tourists, a few couples here and there, and a man with one of those gilded Venetian masks covering his eyes. He had a small entourage accompanying him, and Sawyer and I wondered who he might be. Maybe royalty, or a Bollywood film star.

Sawyer and I settled at our table and surveyed the dishes before us. Wide ceramic platters filled with bloody haunches of meat—partridge, venison, and apricot-stuffed turkey—served as main courses to all sorts of pastries, some with whole birds baked inside, as well as lemon tarts and stuffed crab apples and purple fruits spiked with green leaves. And interspersed between these were hundreds of tiny dishes with toasted nuts, bread knots with jam, and mussels, perfect pea pods and miniature beets and dumpling squash all poached and caramelized, toasted eel strips and marmalade drops, twenty-five varieties of sugared lavender, and chutney, and cream puffs, and pickled snapper fish, and smoky cheesecakes, and platters of silkworm noodles, and exquisite little nutmeg buns, and chili crème fraiche and saucy ribs, plus jugs of wine, and carafes of liquor thick with fruit, not to mention a kind of aphrodisiac milk-tea.

Seeing all this, Sawyer and I first shared a look of disbelief and then shrugged and grinned and started to eat. No order or sense was apparent. We just ate from one plate then another, feeding each other, cooing at some new discovery or going back for another bite or sip from something already tasted. It was a sensory experience like none I'd had before, not even with Philip at his preposterous meals, which now seemed restrained in comparison.

As we ate, we heard the music from a small chamber orchestra composed solely of silver-haired women wearing silver dresses. After an extended number, they took a break and lounged for a few minutes in a gazebo set inside a garden of tulips. Eating paper-thin wafers twisted like ties, and sipping mint and lemon and ice crush from thin flute glasses, they appeared thoroughly at home. Toward the end of their break, another woman joined them.

"Is that Laralee?" I asked Sawyer.

He paused over a ganache and looked closely. "You're right, it is." She started to sing a song from her new movie while the silver ladies did backup.

After Laralee left, the music became hypnotic. A fountain rose from the floor, spouting water at its center. Suddenly, light shone into the eaves. Above the crowd stood an acrobat wearing a red silk leotard, with yellow hair hanging to her lower back. She was poised to perform.

She leaped into empty air and caught two hoops hanging from the ceiling. She swung round and round over herself, faster and faster, curving in serpent-like trails around her own body and the hoops. All at once, she dove again into mid-air—into nothing it seemed—and zoomed downward toward the fountain. Disappearing into the bubbling water, she rose a few moments later upon a platform that surfaced from the spray, some primitive sea creature rising from the depths of the ocean. Fully emerged, she started dancing between the tables.

And all this time we ate with our fingers and sipped from different gourds, and the blurring effect of the food made us lean into each other, sensing our bodies in a slow-motion, visceral way. I kept looking at Sawyer and wondered: Did he feel as alive and as free as I felt?

And it was like that, too, when we came home and fell as one body onto my bed.

Sawyer pulled back for a second. "Do you want this?"

"What do you mean?" I sighed, unwilling to be drawn out of the place where I was disappearing. "Yes, of course." For a moment, Sawyer had a faraway look. Then it was gone. And we were both desperate and timeless.

"Don't you think it was all leading to this?" Sawyer murmured afterward into my tangled hair. I closed my eyes as he took my hand and then moved closer to him. Later, Sawyer drifted off but I could not sleep. I studied the contour of his long limbs stretched across the mattress. He looked young—maybe too young for me—and I felt young too, young and keen. And I marveled at what was unfolding between us, so different from my relationship with Jack, one which had always been fixed and mechanical from the start. But this was something different, something suspenseful that moved from one unknowable moment to the next. I curled up onto his chest, wondering what would come of it.

The next morning when I woke, Sawyer was already up. He stood in the corner of my bedroom, watching me sleep. Fully dressed, his hair spiked from the pillow and the lines of crumpled sheets still faint on his cheek, he seemed embarrassed and brooding but unable to bring himself to leave.

I sat up in bed. "What's wrong?"

"I should go."

"Why?"

He shook his head, as if trying to clear it. "I have work to do."

I pulled the sheets around me, digging into them for my clothing. I extended one hand to him. He came closer, reluctantly, and took it. And once he was touching me, he seemed to soften. "It's okay," I said.

His shoulders sagged. "I suppose I don't have to go just yet."

I jumped up. "Just come with me for coffee."

At the coffee shop, we found a table in the back corner. Over coffee and scones, we each went off into our own worlds. Sawyer wore headphones and tapped on a borrowed notepad. I poured over Penny's poem revisions. *There's something here,* I wrote into the margin of one poem, *but you're too interested in the shock value. Go deeper.* This was something I had written to her on several other drafts.

I looked over at Sawyer. He was so beautiful that I couldn't believe he was with me. I made a gesture. He lowered his headphones and stopped scribbling notes a moment. "God, just being around you makes my head buzz," I told him. "It's good for my work." I put a hand on his arm. "I guess that officially makes you my muse."

"I think you've just had too much coffee." He smiled. "But I'm flattered anyway."

I'd never had a muse before. To be fair, in the early days, Jack had tried to participate in my writing. He would ask to read my work sometimes, if only bits and pieces, and he would get excited on my behalf when I was seized with an idea. But the more I spoke, the more his interest thinned, and that powerful exchange was just not there with him; so instead of charging me, it drained me. Anyway, as the years went by, and my writing projects fizzled, and my own excitement darkened, it changed.

Under the table as we worked, I stretched one foot and rested it on Sawyer's chair across from me. Now and then, while he paused to calculate in his writing, he clasped the pen between his teeth and wrapped a hand around my ankle, almost absentmindedly. Somewhere into the second pot of coffee, without any fanfare, we decided to see a movie that night, as if we had been together for years.

Lena texted me: *Cancellation tomorrow night. Up for something interesting?*

"Aren't you exhausted from yesterday?" Sawyer shook his head and laughed when I asked him if we should go. "And stuffed? Not sure if I can handle another round of that. Can you?"

"It will be another room, a totally different experience. And it's not until tomorrow, anyway," I promised him.

He shrugged then touched my cheek. "Prongs tomorrow, but today we can just take it easy. No Saudi kings. No naked ladies. No goose liver."

Even before he finished speaking, I began a return text to Lena: *On for tomorrow.*

11.

"Are you game?" Lena asked me and Sawyer the next night. "I mean really game."

Sawyer gave a small grimace and peered anxiously at the silver chain door before us. He raised an eyebrow at me.

"He means yes," I told her.

"You have to give yourself completely to the organics hall." She smiled mischievously. "Otherwise it's just bizarre."

Lena had taken me in for Philip's sake, and by now she seemed to like me well enough. But more and more I could see she also had some real glee—or was it a belligerent pride?—in showing me the spectacles of Prongs. Like taking a spinster aunt out for a raunchy night downtown.

She punched the buttons to open the door and led us into a space that was a simple grass clearing around a smoky fire pit. A small stream wound its way through the middle of the circle and the ceiling above had the look of a nearly dark sky with stars emerging. We sat on the floor, which had a soft boggy smell, as if it had been built over marshland, and leaned against boulders that were designed to curve into rock chaises.

Two wild looking men walked by with trenches of food. "I think they're our waiters," I said in a hushed tone.

Barefoot and wearing nothing but animal skins, the men had straggly hair and cheeks painted in rusty colors. They did not speak, but gestured with their hands. Their grunts seemed crude and primeval.

The painted people brought one of the big wooden trenches to us, overflowing with mounds of raw plants. There were no utensils, and around the circle other patrons started to pick at the food with their hands. There were feathered greens that looked like they grew wild in fields, stalks and roots that had been snapped out of the earth only moments ago, tart berries and tiny bulbs and herbs. Everything tasted fresh and untouched. "Salad," Sawyer announced brightly, digging in. He seemed relieved at the simplicity of it.

Daniel himself came out of the kitchen to check on us as the painted people walked round with animal skins of water for each of us. "Taste the water," he told me proudly. "It's my special recipe: mountain water from underground springs gently churned for twenty-four hours in lava rocks, and then chilled right before serving in icicles that formed all winter long on lemon trees in my own garden." He took a sip from his skin of water and nodded. "If you close your eyes and imagine the lemon grove, you can probably taste a hint of citrus." He swirled another mouthful, concentrating with each taste bud. "But this batch also has a bright, buttery layer to it, and a surprising steely feel in the finish. Just like wine, every batch is its own creature," he mused.

Instead of entertainment, the room highlighted the natural elements. The sky was filled with stars and we located the constellations, and once they were mostly accounted for, we made up our own. Breathtakingly real, the stars twinkled unceasingly, and one or two even seemed to fall now and then, so we gazed in anticipation of catching sight of some far-off world collapsing upon itself.

The stream of water now bubbled more forcefully through the center of our circle, and the room was chillier so we leaned toward the heat of the fire, watching the flames in their endless moving sculpture.

Stars, water, and fire might have seemed so commonplace, but before there were other diversions, hadn't people lived under their spell for thousands of years? Hadn't they inspired countless forms of worship? Here was Lena's genius, I marveled, in channeling that ancient draw so exactly.

Later, Sawyer said there must have been something else, some herb in the salad, or perhaps some powder thrown onto the fragrant fire so the smoke enhanced our senses. Understanding a little about how the place operated behind the scenes, I knew he was right. A concoction from Jill's lab was clearly at work. But I stopped myself from speculating. And time seemed to pass differently, moving as it did from gush to glimpse, and when we grew hungry again, it was a senseless raging hunger.

The painted people appeared with great round wooden platters, each so large that it took two people to balance it between them. An enormous spongy pancake covered the entire wooden surface, but it was barely visible for the mounds of stewed foods that covered it. Each mound was distinct in scent and color.

Ravenous, I tore off a triangle of the pancake, folded it around a thick red gruel, like some biblical lentil soup. I pinched the entire pocket into my mouth. It woke up my throat. A moment later, I seemed to feel it seeping through my tissues.

"What is that?" I asked Sawyer.

He tried it, too. "I have no idea."

"It's not that it's spicy." I took another mouthful of water. "I mean, it is spicy. But there's also a flavor that I've never tasted before."

"You're right. I can't place it either." Sawyer made himself another pocket, this time from a mustard-like mash. "This one is delicious, too, but it's almost like it's not even food."

"I'm pretty sure we are eating something horrific," I told him finally.

He agreed. But in the heat of the feast, we laughed it off because it tasted good, and we felt uninhibited and so, so hungry. We ate and ate from everything on the platter, until our stomachs finally came into balance again with our perceptions.

After that initial rush, Sawyer and I settled against the boulders to catch our breaths. I noticed Lena in a corner speaking with a party of patrons. When she was finished and about to leave, I motioned to her.

"Should I even ask what all this food actually is?" I pointed to our platter with the shredded pancake, and each stew diminished.

"Most people don't want to know," she laughed. "They come, as if this was sky-diving or swimming with sharks—just to be pushed out of their comfort zones. Afterward, the palette is forever changed." She cast one arm around the room. "And then, nothing is taboo, nothing is off limits."

"*I* want to know." I put a hand on her shoulder. "Tell me."

She leaned toward me, lowering her voice conspiratorially. "Forget Paris: this is where Daniel's real genius shines." She pointed to the mound closest to her on the platter. "Fermented garlic pureed with a cheese aged in a beer barrel of maggots, and fried bits of free-choice organic human bacon." She pointed to the next one. "Minced duck embryo in good soil, shallots, and chili oil." Beside me, Sawyer groaned. "Coconut milk with a pinch of dried dung flakes, infused with lavender oil and a grassy syrup."

"Stop," Sawyer groaned. He looked angry, as if discovering he had been tricked. "I don't want to hear anymore."

"Suit yourself." Lena shrugged a bit in disdain and walked away. He didn't eat another bite after that. And I was more hesitant, too. But then they brought out a honey tart topped by the lightest crust and feathered with finely ground gold bullion and black salt. And since I was curious, I tried just a bite, which was so wonderful that I finished the whole thing myself. And then I had enough room left for a handful of the crisped caterpillars peppered with cinnamon, like mixed nuts. And I ended the night drinking a carafe of thinned blood and grapefruit vodka.

"The truth is," I told Sawyer on the way home, linking one arm in his. "It wasn't bad. And actually, it was pretty damn good. We just have these hang-ups. And that's what Prongs is about, pushing limits."

He shook his head in disgust. He seemed to be getting more and more wound up as we walked away from Prongs, as if the air outside was clearing his mind. "Listen, if you have to eat insects, you have to eat insects. You do what you do to survive. Where I grew up, people ate squirrels. Sometimes they ate roadkill. But if you have everything—I mean, if you can get a perfectly good sandwich right down the street, why wouldn't you?"

"Come on."

"No, really, what is it with this obsession for the most grotesque thing possible?"

I tried to reason with him. "It goes beyond that."

He peered at me like he didn't fully recognize me. "I just don't understand people." He had a look of bewilderment on his face, and a bit of disgust, too. But I was thoroughly caught up in Prongs. If only he could understand this new world of food as I was starting to understand it, to see the beauty in what humans might imagine, and what they might concoct. Then would he be truly alive, truly changed. "Free-choice organic human bacon: What does that even mean?"

"You don't believe it's free choice?" I spoke deliberately, hoping if I slowed all this down, we would be allies again.

"I don't know, let's say it *is* free choice. What could possibly be behind making a choice like that? Come on. Everything about that place." He did some calculations in his head. "I'd guess the hundred or so people down there tonight probably paid ten thousand dollars a head to be there. Ten thousand dollars for a few hours! That spending, that waste. That bacon. It's all unimaginable."

"You're right," I said, gripping his jacket. "The waste is sickening. But what a feat, too. It was like walking through a perfectly orchestrated opera. You know?"

We neared the station near Purr where there was a train that could take me to my house. He stopped abruptly and my stomach fell. "Aren't you coming back with me?" I asked cautiously.

He caught himself and spoke evenly. "I really need to get this proposal done by tomorrow."

For a moment I felt myself panic. I had been stringing my world back into order, stitch by stitch, around him. But suddenly it all seemed like it could collapse. Everything had been happening through Prongs and Lena and cricket flour crepes and butchering your own rabbit. I had assumed that, like me, Sawyer wanted to be reborn. I saw suddenly that he did not. I held the solid curve of his arm a moment too long. "I'll see you tomorrow though, right?"

Where had that come from so suddenly, me expecting time together, and so completely folding him in? Sure, we'd been sending loaded text messages to each other for weeks now, but it had been only a matter of seventy-two hours, more or less, since we'd been anything more than friends. I bit my lip. I had forgotten that unnatural suspense of being together intimately, vulnerable, even while still sizing each other up.

"Yes, tomorrow." He took my face in his hands. It looked like he wanted to kiss me but then he stopped. "I'll meet you early at that coffee shop—the one around the corner from your place."

"Okay." I softened and leaned into him a little. That could be good. I loved early mornings. The streets would be empty as I walked, arriving just when the coffee shop opened. I would settle in at the table near the counter while they turned on the lights and fired up the coffee machines. I would see the behind-the-scenes intricacies as they set up shop: trucks coming into the city from the farms to make vegetable deliveries; pastries coming out of the ovens, the cafe's tiny civilization forming in fast-forward.

"We can work there," Sawyer added.

I pulled back. "Work again?"

"Work again," he repeated, as if staking a claim, as if daring me to question it. But I could tell from the look on his face that it was not a list of tasks or labor that he was talking about. He was talking about routine, clinging to the steady tedium of it. I knew because during all those years with Jack, carrying out the quiet routines of our household, I had clung to it, too. Now, I could not imagine why.

I drew back. "What's the new work proposal all about?" I finally asked him, squaring off near the stairs that led to the subway station.

He lifted his chin. "*Potential...* Nothing guaranteed. I'm just assessing what kind of soundtrack might work for this group."

"What group?"

"You wouldn't know them."

"What do they do? " I pushed.

He sighed. "It's a bunch of different religious groups, working to promote what they have in common."

"Like pro-life clinics, and unseen women?" I shook my head in disbelief. "What are you doing?"

"No. They're complicated." He crossed his arms in front of him. "It's not stuffing girls into hijabs and aprons. They want to make the world better."

"I'll bet," I muttered, shaking my head. "Come on. That's not your thing."

"I'm not sure you're one to talk," he told me coldly. "Didn't we just eat actual shit for whatever it is that's your 'thing'?"

"What's the connection?" I threw up my hands. "Sawyer, you didn't major in Music Studies so you could do this." I made myself calm down. "Back in college, everyone, even the faculty who really knew what they were talking about, everyone said you were a genius. Do you know how amazing it was when you got up at that little bar and played guitar the other night? What are you doing?"

This hit a nerve. "Look, it's a job. People need to work." He searched further, defensively. "Also, they're not what you think?"

"How so?" I braced myself to try to treat this as an intellectual discussion.

"You know better. You can't lump everything together into some sweeping extremism."

"Maybe." Perhaps he was right. But something else still gnawed at me.

"Trust me on this," he said.

"Look, what I'm doing right now isn't so much better, really. Stupid coupons. And some random classes. But I'm also not *okay* with it." This was where I got stuck. "You? You're fine just floating."

He couldn't deny it, this was truth. He reached for me with one hand, to include me in the floating. But I backed away. Without another word, he turned sharply and walked toward his bus. Numbly, I turned too and walked down the subway stairs.

I found myself on the crowded train platform, looking at the faces of everyone packed together. It suddenly seemed so clear, our collective unimportance: We all want to be convinced of our uniqueness and our magic, and we look yearningly to nature for assurance; no two snowflakes exactly alike, no wave folds or falls exactly the same. But over billions of years, and of the number of snowflakes that have fallen to earth, and all the waves that have crashed upon a single shore, certainly there have existed many so very alike that any actual difference is rendered meaningless.

That grim anonymity, I decided, if we let it, that could be the sum of our human pursuit after all. And it seemed clearer to me now on the subway platform than it ever had above ground.

12.

I climbed back up the subway stairs and headed toward The Quarter on foot, passing the farmers' market and Prongs and then Purr. Leaving behind the most exterior streets and the perimeter that I knew, I went deeper into a new area. It seemed to be a tiny Paris, housing The Quarter's French restaurants and producers. A sign proclaimed that the area boasted nearly the same status as a foreign embassy, and that the producers of bubbly wine and soft cheese here could market their products using the officially guarded French titles. It was pretty but I was not very impressed. Many tourists flocked there, just the way people who went to Disney's Epcot descended on its mini landmarks, as though they were the real things. I saw the kitschy beret vendors and crepe stands, the pavilion constructed to resemble the underbelly of the Eiffel Tower, the roving street musicians. For some reason, with Paris of all places, people could not distinguish the cliché from the essence. And tourists from the Midwest strolled hand in hand taking pictures by the faux Eiffel Tower without any sense of irony, dropping money into the musician's cup as though he were not just someone hired by The Quarter's corporate office, but a true, struggling musician hoping for his big break on the streets of Paris.

I quickly bypassed the big glamorous restaurants, the French wine and buttery snails and all the kitsch of Paris, looking for something else. According to Philip, the simple pleasure of acquiring and consuming food itself was almost obsolete at night here anyway. The process was everything now, he told me, and especially after dark it was all about the Makers in what they called the night market. Every now and then, there would be a raid on this part of The Quarter that made the papers, and people would rally to clean up its underground scene or picket that it had gotten out of control. But mostly it was a wild frontier of earnest Makers and opportunistic gangsters, and everything in between.

I trailed further away from the most commercial area and passed under a lit-up archway. I followed the meandering side streets, courtyards, and plazas and soon everywhere I went I found what he had described: places for just about any kind of food production experience where people could not only witness but also partake in the essential act of creation. Walking past storefronts, or peering through the frosted glass of a shop, I saw chocolate-makers at their craft, bakers grinding their own acorn flour, a butcher carving a pig with customers at the bar drinking warm shots of fresh blood as they discussed technique. Authentic process—people getting their hands dirty—that's what foodies sought out come night.

During the day, this area was quiet, with most of the storefronts shuttered. But now, splattered sidewalks showed signs of the rowdy nightlife, where the whiskey distillers worked, and the winemakers tended their cellars, and the beer brewers taught their art to eager students. One long window showed people sitting on stools waiting to be summoned like living confections from behind the glass. Beneath each seat was a printed card detailing what the person could officially offer. *Milk cows with an actual farm girl*, it said beneath one girl, her hair in thick cartoon braids. *Barefoot grape stomping*. This girl had long black hair that roped around her waist. Her bare feet, stained purple, swung from the stool where she sat, as she seemed to assess each person who passed. Below a slender and pretty Polynesian man wearing eyeliner: *Maori cooking in the true indigenous tradition*. And then another: *Hand-make tortillas with a Mexicana*. The girl on this stool was barefoot, too. But she looked no older than twelve, and bewildered, or maybe stoned. A couple lingered at the glass and the manager came out. "Does something interest you?"

I walked further into the district, turned down Main Street, and passed a cheese-maker. A young, bearded man in the glass front lovingly tended a deep milky vat the length of the window. Pausing to adjust his glasses, he spotted me and beamed, then gave a peace sign with two gloved fingers.

I passed a Mediterranean butcher. Built like a souk, the store was scattered with all kinds of foliage, branches of olive and date trees with hard budded fruit, tiny oranges with lush green leaves still clinging to their twigs, grape vines spilling purple. The smell of spices in open bins wafted out of an aqua-tiled archway, mixing with the smell of raw flesh. Further back in sing-song, the vendor chanted about the merits of the fresh meats in his cases: "Boned, diced, halal, spiced!"

Next-door was a vintage clothing shop. Faceless naked female mannequins in the window wore authentic burro harnesses used to transport grains in Mexico. I walked into a store called Workshop, which seemed to sell kitchen tools. The bell above the door clanged and I peeked down a hallway into a maze of tiny workshops, class-rooms, and studios. In one room they were blowing glass, in anoth-er they were crafting knives, banging out heated steel over the fire.

"How can I help you?" The shop owner came out and introduced himself. "No, wait. Don't tell me. My gift is that I know what a cook needs even before she does!" His shop had shelves and shelves of boxes with the most peculiar and particular gadgets that he had either made or discovered somewhere: wine glasses with bottle open-ers on the base, chopsticks made from every imaginable material, salt lamps, ancient tea sets, Marilyn Monroe china plates. It was endless.

"I'm just looking," I told him, before he could size me up and try to sell me something.

Walking down another alley, I passed a cookbook store, which was having a sale. On the corner was a new upscale restaurant devot-ed solely to olives. There was a Seed Library with thousands of small wooden drawers that contained seeds from all over the world for gardeners with boxes hanging out their kitchen windows. A corner shop housed a goat whisperer, where someone seemed to be teach-ing young milk aficionados the art of massage which would yield the creamiest milk. I saw a spa called Delicious, where a sign advertised that one could spend two entire days rolled up in honey comb while sipping a diluted, therapeutic honey from a tube. Afterward, your skin would look like you were ten years old again, it promised.

Later I discovered a laboratory of sorts, where a white-smocked and bespectacled man paced in front of the window before a few students. They also wore white smocks. A counter was lined with microscopes. Nearby sat a contraption of glass spheres filled with different colored liquids, and near that, a fish, clipped and suspended upside down to be gutted soon. The teacher held up a fat red lobster, its claws wrapped in rubber bands, like tiny silk-bound feet. He approached a large boiling pot and dropped the lobster into it, then craned forward with one hand cupped over his ear. The students leaned forward too, all listening for noises coming from the pot, scribbling notes and trying to decide whether it was merely the sound of bubbles expanding into the spaces of the claws, or the tortured cries of an animal.

Next door was a connected space, presumably run by the same pop scientist, with a glass ceiling and a teeming biosphere inside. A sign overhead read: *Eden.* Carpets of thick wild grass, patches of ancient red clay, and fruit trees heavy with fruit—everywhere leaves cascading down to form shiny green and purple curtains. The steaming mix of stream water running through it, a sign explained, was said to have the environmental effect of the Tigris and Euphrates rivers. It was lovely, lush and flowery and I could almost smell jasmine through the window. I pressed my nose against the glass, wondering if this was indeed how Eden had looked. Was it possible to go inside?

I looked for a door but the biosphere was apparently not for public use. Maybe it was used to grow herbs for experiments. Or was it simply to draw people into the workshops? I stopped short. At the center of the garden were two brown humans, absolutely naked and apparently asleep for the night. They appeared perfectly at home, as if they had never known shoes or clothing or food that they hadn't picked themselves. I peered at them for a while but they didn't stir so I tiptoed away and continued down the street.

On the same block was an apothecary with all kinds of medicinal ingredients in blue and green and yellow bottles lined up in front of the window. Further on was a smokehouse where they only used hand-hewn wood chips and artisanal coals to cure their meats. At Chile Depot a group of goggled students sat at a bar learning about the variety of peppers. A Buttermilk Stand offered a buttermilk bourbon which was very popular at weddings, but the sign in front boasted that they could help customers craft a one-of-a-kind buttermilk for any occasion.

I crossed the street to look into a window where a sign above the door read: Fortune Teller. Through the glass I could see a plump old lady with her hair wrapped in a bejeweled turban. She held the hand of an elegant woman, probably from the upper eastside, and seemed to speak to her earnestly. *We conjure up the dead,* a sign outside read, *and their lost recipes, too.*

At a nearby ice cream shop two men stood behind the counter—one of those old-fashioned wooden ice boxes with the word *ice* etched into the painted side. One of the men saw me. "Welcome," he led me further into the store and pointed to a stool.

"Exactly what kind of ice cream shop is this?" I peered through chilled glass at rows and rows of silvered bonbons, each unique.

"We make one-of-a-kind ice cream bonbons." One of the men tied on an apron and opened the case. Indeed, the bonbons were actually spherical ice cream cubes. Some had flower petals, some tiny peppercorns, others mint leaves and clover. "You seem like eventually you could handle a cicada ice cream." He grinned. "But for now, I'll start you off with a simple Thames variety—water purified just outside London and a hint of sweet cream and organic young grass from the Kingston countryside." He placed the sphere onto a tiny plate. Frosty bits of grass were caught within.

"Go ahead." The other man urged me, stroking his goatee in gleeful expectation. "Just let it melt in your mouth."

I placed it on my tongue and the cold, green-tasting cream thawed as it went down my throat in a perfect, surprising cascade. "Who would have thought that ice cream could be such an art?" I swept a hand, still somewhat bewildered, over the room.

"Bonbons are just the beginning." The man closed the case again. "We build ice cream sculptures, teach mixology and proper tasting technique." He walked me to a freezer at the back of the store, opened the walk-in door and led me inside. "Here we have the royalty." He flung up the corner of a wax paper tarp and unveiled a great block of ice cream, beneath it a bloody haunch of beef, its perfect ruby color marbled with pearly fat veins. And it was sandwiched by another great block of ice cream. He crooked his hands in his overalls, allowing me to take it all in. "The beef is a marvelous cut, too, from a beautiful red cow. But it's the ice cream blocks themselves that are really prime. Refined water from the Dead Sea, mixed with the cream of the cow's own mother's milk and studded with peppercorns. She's been nestled between these blocks since slaughter. Anything you can think of with ice cream, that's what we do here," they assured me as I left the store. I was somehow amazed by the whimsy of this place, delighting that such a simple thing as ice cream could be so celebrated.

As the door closed behind me, I thought about Sawyer. No, Sawyer would not appreciate a place like this—not at all, I realized—he would give that old grin and call it the Emperor's New Clothes or something, and because of this I understood there was no hope for him, and no hope for us.

I made my way back into the more trafficked part of The Quarter, where people sat outside in booths and shared platters of food that were like great sprawling sculptures: pyramids of avocado toast, the giant triangles of bread pocked with seeds and thick pink salt crystals. And caramelized fairytale eggplants, still purple and stuffed with nuts and fruit and cheese, positioned like cherubs in the center of the plate. And there were extra-large pitchers of peach sangria that seemed like they had been drawn for a cartoon, too big for mere mortals.

Looking for another surprise, I turned down a narrow alley. As I made my way through it, the alley circled around and around. The old buildings were thick here and had been played up during renovation to feel like an ancient port city, Acre or Istanbul, burrowed into a cliff, the walls and winding streets and millennia-old rock all one and the same. Within a few minutes I was lost.

Then up ahead, where the alley turned, I saw two or three people entering the ornate doorway of a place that might have once been a church—gargoyles above it with small panes of stained glass, but only a low-watt bulb now lit the arch. Following those before me, I opened the door quickly and slipped inside.

I entered into a cavernous room with long plain tables striping it up and down. Men, as far as the eye could see, sat huddled at the tables. They wore drab brown linen, purposely plain. They read books and parchments and scribbled notes, all the while in separate conversations that together formed a low but constant din making it almost impossible to hear any one voice.

I walked between two tables and stopped behind one man who was speaking earnestly, his body rocking rhythmically the whole time. "Excuse me," I said. He didn't hear me. "Excuse me," I said again and tapped his shoulder.

The touch seemed to stop every conversation in the room at once. The man I had approached froze and kept his eyes locked on the text in front of him. The man across from him, with whom he had been deep in conversation, looked up with a withering glance, distant and detached, as if he had somehow been woken rudely from dreaming.

"Excuse me," I said now into the general silence of the room, "I'm trying to get back to the main Quarter. Is there anyone here who can direct me?"

No one spoke. After several moments, a man rose at the other end of the room and walked toward me. Barefoot and bearded, he seemed like the leader of the group, with a lean, magnetic energy and shining, warm eyes. As soon as he reached me, the noise again broke out around us.

"My apologies," he said as he led me toward a small office near the entrance. He pointed me to a seat at the table. "Our people do not see many others here, not even our own women. So manners can be a bit rusty."

I took a seat, relieved to rest after my wandering and the strange encounter in the big hall. "What is this place? Who are you?"

"I'm Robby, the teacher here. This place is our humble little retreat at the edge of The Quarter." He lowered himself onto the seat across from me. "Seems like an ordinary spot, doesn't it? But as the story goes, this building occupies the ground where an inn once stood, and where George Washington once dined as he made his way up the Hudson. There have supposedly been pewter spoons unearthed from that time, pieces of the original table at the inn. These days though," he smiled, "it's just a place where people can run to if they need a sanctuary. And goodness knows, The Quarter has its share of runaways."

"Running from what?" I looked around. "To what?"

He sighed. "I offer the disenchanted a chance to be whole again, to learn a new way. That's what we are doing here."

I doubted that even Philip knew of this place but if he did, I was certain, he would have warned to me steer clear. *Of course,* I could practically hear him mocking in my head. *Leave it to you to go out for a perfectly nice night on the town…and come home shackled to some cult.* But still I had to ask, "What is the learning?"

Robby stroked his beard slowly between thumb and pointer. "Many years ago, I used to learn in a place just like this, a place of men and faith and texts. In New City," he chuckled to himself. "Can you imagine? Somewhere, though, I fell off the path. And though I must have learned the laws of kashrus for thousands of hours, one day, months later, I woke up and I found myself eating ham sandwiches and cheeseburgers. And not just eating them, but gorging until long after I was already stuffed, cramming food into my mouth over the kitchen sink, or in an alley behind some restaurant, till I felt sick. I went from one extreme to the other. I was so very, very lost." I leaned forward, anxious to hear more. "But eventually I started to see the wisdom of the prohibition on ham, not so much for the ham, but for the prohibition itself, and the restraint. And then I looked at other faiths and other ways, and I realized that over centuries people have collected their greatest wisdom in the laws of food. So here we do not worship food as they do out there." He nodded toward The Quarter. "And we do not worship one faith or any single way of sustenance. Rather we have collected the wisdom of food in all civilizations, and that is what we seek to understand."

I stood and moved toward the door that opened to the large room beyond. Robby stood behind me. "So what exactly are they studying?"

He pointed to a young man in tight-wire glasses at the nearest table who read aloud from a page, one finger tracing the text line by line. "He has been here just under six months. Today he is learning about how lettuce is forbidden among certain sects because it was pelted at a Saint bound for execution. *The leaf of humiliation.*"

I edged back into the larger room, and could now, among the mass of tables, start to isolate individual conversations. A group of old men sat around a table. "How much flesh is forbidden?" one asked. "The size of an olive?" He measured it out, holding two cracked fingers apart.

The others nodded gravely. "No more than 1/60 of the full pot."

I walked amidst small conversations, different groups of men discussing Lent, halal and haram, the forbidden slaughterhouse of female cows, prohibitions on caffeine and alcohol, and eggs with blood spots on them or just any eggs at all. Often the groups of men resembled each other in some way, older together and younger together, those who looked like they had been hipsters or those lost and unable to make it on the outside, all somehow newly reconfigured in those same circles here, with others like themselves.

Up and down the table were different discussions: "If you don't eat grains, can you marry someone who does?"

Further down I heard, "It simply says do not cook a calf in its mother's milk." The man pointed to a text in Hebrew. "But all these fences that guard this prohibition? Cooking meat and dairy in separate dishes. Waiting several hours after eating the meat before eating the dairy, and only after washing the mouth, and only when the meat has been slaughtered and stamped by an expert." He held up a finger. "It is almost as if the more complicated, the better."

And at the next table, another man asked, "Doesn't eating a root vegetable kill the whole plant? Then it, too, is an act of destruction."

Another student seated nearby, an anxious, impatient type, put a hand on the teacher's arm as we passed. "Robby," he said plaintively, a bit bug-eyed and eager for knowledge, "when will I know everything I can know here?"

The teacher stopped a moment to face him and nodded deeply, thinking. "You will know everything when you can explain to me how the ancient writings tell of two people who eat a fish together. When the meal is finished, one is hungry, with his hands full of scales and grease. The other is full, but clean. Tell me, how can that be?"

The student scratched his head for a moment. "Perhaps the hungry person is the servant who has prepared the food, the full person is his master who has eaten it." Robby shook his head. "Okay. Then maybe," the student went on, "the hungry one is actually a baby who played with his food, scattering it here and there. The mother who cleaned up after him and ate the scraps herself is full." Before Robby could even say anything, the student countered himself. "Unless, the important clue is that the two people ate together. Only two equals can eat together, which is neither servant and master, nor mother and child."

"So what is your answer?" Robby asked.

But the student could only continue circling. He stood up, grasping at straws. "One person was greasy and full of scales, and though some law requires the presence of scales on fish, who would eat a fish with its scales instead of cleaning it before eating?" He was desperate now, hands up in resignation. "But are the scales even important? Does it at all matter that it's a fish?"

Robby put a gentle hand on the student's shoulder, to calm him. "Don't you see? There were scales but there were no fins. The law says both scales *and* fins," the teacher added, almost sadly. "And yet, two people ate a fish together. When they finished, one was hungry and soiled, the other full but clean. So how can it be? And they were in the desert—see, you did not even ask where they were—no sea for many thousands of miles around. So how could they eat fish if there were no fish in the first place?" Robby tapped his own skull lightly. "The fish itself," he told the student, now humbled, "that was the illusion."

The student eased back into his seat as we moved away from the table. "I sense," Robby finally said after a few moments, "that our study here interests you."

"It does," I admitted.

"We have women's groups too, you know," he assured me. "They learn more practicalities, less theory. But if you wish it, there would be a place at our table for you." I had been in this moment before, maybe many times. When I didn't answer, he prodded. "Can it be just chance that of all the places in The Quarter, you came to our doorstep tonight?"

I nodded, acknowledging that the coincidence was compelling.

"We're like a family here; we rely mostly on each other." He pointed out the window that looked onto the backyard of the building. "Something new this year…" It was a space that was once a parking lot, and still had tall hooded lights and gates circling the perimeter. Lit up, I could see the expanse clearly, where a number of people gathered, hard at work. "Everyone puts in their time, each according to his abilities." All the cement had nearly been torn up and now only the hard soil beneath lay bared. "Come spring, we'll make a garden. Come five years, we'll be entirely self-sufficient." One of the workers approached the back door and came inside, hands and fingernails grubby, cheeks pink from exertion. He washed his hands at the sink and then filled a bowl of rice to eat with the others.

Robby and I moved further along the back wall. In one area a small group of men meditated. In the most remote corner beyond them a few men gathered around a woven basket with some excitement. I drew nearer, Robby still alongside me.

Each man seated himself around the basket, and then one of them removed the top. A poisonous snake rose up slowly, pointed and sinister, wavering in the same charmer's dance often seen in the movies.

"What the hell?" I startled forward but then drew back with a shudder.

Anticipating my reaction, Robby moved with confidence. "Don't worry. You're safe. People don't sit with the snakes until they are ready."

"Ready?" I shook my head, still unsettled. "You control snakes?"

"No," Robby said in a hushed tone. "But we do know that eating the reptile is in many cultures forbidden. So we study the serpent to try and understand this, to look into its eyes and see what men fear and why."

I watched in awe as they now tried to stare down the snake. The man who had removed the basket top was probably Robby's most senior pupil, his deputy. With one hand he signaled to the men around him to watch. And he drew closer to the snake, head cocked as he studied its dangerous moves, parrying with it in an ever-bolder dance. One of the men in the group, a frail boy really, seemed especially intent. He watched the deputy with wondering eyes and mimicked his movements. I saw his lips move, but just barely, repeating what the man had said, under his breath so he could learn it by heart. It was a beautiful thing, almost a private moment, to watch that transmission of knowledge.

And then I remembered something that I had seen on the streets in India, a moment almost exactly like this one, a man dancing with a cobra in complete and inexplicable confidence—only possible because the creature was defanged. I straightened, understanding it clearly now. "Do they know that the snake can't bite them?"

Robby spread his hands, palms open and elevated in praise of both the end and the means. He closed his eyes to acknowledge the truth. "No. They don't know."

"But I do."

To my surprise, though, his admission lifted me: The pursuit of purpose was a wondrous thing. Nodding, I turned toward the exit.

13.

Next morning, as I drank my coffee, I stopped every few minutes to rub ointment onto the muscles of my legs. All that walking the night before—through The Quarter for hours and hours and then all the way home—had left me aching. At some point Aiden lumbered down the stairs, grunting. He poured himself a bowl of cereal and milk. He perched at the table one seat away from me, and ate spoonful after spoonful, reading something on his phone screen. Now and then, he stopped to type something with his thumbs, or send a message, and then he went back to reading.

I massaged my thighs, then my calves. And as the smell of menthol wafted through the room, it was very quiet, breaking only with the sound of his crunching and the random scrape of spoon against bowl. Suddenly, I noticed the quiet moments lengthening into minutes, and it seemed absurd that we just sat there without talking. Aiden did not look up, did not stop his motion between spoon, bowl, and screen.

I could have asked my usual parent questions and received his usual half-syllable answers. But instead I was struck that the lack of human contact between two people within a few feet of each other didn't seem to bother him. Perhaps it was just teenage sullenness, but I knew that the silence had expanded since the divorce, and particularly since I'd returned from India.

"Aiden." I set aside the tube of ointment. He didn't answer. "Aiden?"

He looked up. "What?"

"What's new?"

He shrugged.

"Do you realize you've been here thirty minutes and haven't said a word?"

"Okay, whatever. Sorry."

"What are you doing there, anyway?"

"Making plans for tonight." He clicked off his phone and stood up, put his bowl and spoon in the sink. "What's the big deal? It's not like you were talking to me either, you know."

"We *can* talk about anything. You know that, right? Is there anything you want to talk about?" I asked carefully, getting up to approach him. Should we talk about the divorce, I wondered in a panic. The idea made me sick. How had I dated some other guy already but was still unable to speak of the divorce with my own son?

As I neared Aiden, I could read his thoughts in his face: *Tell me what happened here, what happened to the three of us?*

But then I saw that he was reading my face, too: *Please. Please don't make me talk about it yet.*

"Nothing," he said, as he walked up the stairs. "I want nothing."

With Sawyer gone, I found myself without plans suddenly. So I kept busy and signed up for Maker classes in The Quarter. First at that ice cream bonbon shop where I experimented making new flavors like a roasted garlic ice cream and then another from lemon curd. The next night I studied under a butcher. Then a weeklong ale workshop.

When I was occupied like that with pleasurable things, it became clear to me that I did not need Sawyer. However, I did, it seemed, need Prongs. I kept thinking about the place, itching to return. After a few days passed, I phoned Lena, thinking maybe she would invite me again. I imagined sitting with her in a magical room that I hadn't seen yet, drinking something purple she had concocted just for me. I would tell her about how it had ended with Sawyer, and she would smile in her way and tell me that that was how it had happened with Sky Walter, too.

But her phone rang on and on and she did not answer; eventually it went to voicemail. I tried again later that day and eventually reached her assistant, who took a message. I never heard back from her.

The following week, I casually mentioned her to Philip as we sat in my office sipping tea. "Have you seen Lena lately?"

He wrinkled his brow. "I thought she was out of town till next week."

"That's right." I nodded, as if remembering too, relieved. Surely she would call me next week then. But she didn't. Maybe something had happened. One night I walked past Purr and then past Prongs, and I stood outside the velvet ropes, hoping she would pass by. But she never did.

Eventually, when more phone calls went unanswered, I assumed it was me, something I had done last time. Or was it Sawyer—because he started to become all prickly at the end, and snappy with the staff? Maybe that was it. I was too embarrassed to admit to Philip that I'd somehow ruined everything with Lena, so I didn't even mention it to him again and thankfully he was too preoccupied wrapping up his film to think to ask.

After I realized I would probably never hear back from Lena, I started missing Sawyer again. More than once I picked up the phone to call him, thinking of how he sang that night at the bar, and the way his voice sounded like whiskey felt going down.

But then I reminded myself that he was not what I had thought. I had made him the unknowing recipient of my own Frankenstein construction, my own belief in a fantasy of him. I scolded myself for falling for our shared history. The older you get, the harder it is to connect to new people. Shared history makes for an instant connection. Not just because you have something in common, but because you want to be with someone who knew you when—when you weren't gray, when you had flushed elastic skin and juicy ideas, when you weren't jaded. If someone looks at you and still sees that, then you can pretend you're still that person too. Phone in hand, I'd remind myself none of it was real.

But mostly I'd remind myself how it felt to be in The Quarter that first night I went in on my own. *That* was real. All the brilliance, that inspiration and pleasure and complexity. So, at the last minute I'd click off the phone and walk to The Quarter instead. It was better that way.

A few weeks later, after taking a tequila workshop in The Quarter, I found myself walking from street to street, amazed again by the place. Beautiful streets in old Jerusalem stone and cobblestone and strung with tiny lights; modern streets with sleek coffee shops and yoga bars behind reflective glass poised in a loop of Enya's music; gritty streets needing to be hosed down every few hours: how was it that such a vast and layered place existed within this city, a second city unto itself?

I walked down a crooked alley and entered a tiny store, nothing more than a scrubbed glassy square, bare-bones but with colorful tour brochures lining pockets along the walls and glossy posters of people at work, grinding, cooking, and mixing. Some offered trips abroad, in the fish markets of Tokyo or to great, exclusive banquets in Delhi. But most were local. I picked up one brochure: *Tuscany in The Quarter,* it read. I picked up another: *Chocolate Tours.* These tours started with bean processing and stopped at a Swiss candy shop, then a hot chocolate bar, and ended at what was once a watch factory, where you could watch the makers create chocolate globes with liquid nitrogen.

There must have been hundreds of different tour brochures. "You're in luck," the woman behind the counter told me. "If you like, there's a tour leaving right now." I didn't even bother asking what kind of tour it was, but I passed her fifteen dollars and she handed me the brochure: a slum tour.

I caught up with the group gathered outside, five Japanese businessmen already taking photos on their cell phones and the guide named Lorne, a scrubbed, freckled activist type, a boyish-looking man, pudgy with thick glasses. He spoke with calm authority. "No photos on this tour, please. We try to respect the dignity of the people in these neighborhoods."

We crossed an intersection on the edge of the eastern district, where the real touristy area ended, and Lorne led us down one road and then another, pointing out more of the offices of infrastructure for the actual residents here. They were disguised somewhat by pretty storefronts, but nonetheless utilitarian: a warehouse for wholesale ingredients; a passport expediter.

As we passed a group of young women standing on the curb at the corner, one of the men started snapping pictures again, but the guide held up a hand. "Please," he scolded. "Let's be respectful."

One of the tourists stopped him. He looked irritated at the lecturing. They should have chosen a tour of Beautiful Women Makers instead, or Noodles, something with no agenda. "What harm could it do?"

"The good people here are objectified enough already. Authentic this, authentic that. They're treated like props. Let's at the least allow them to walk home from work in peace." The man did not seem convinced. So Lorne pointed at some tin structures nearby that served as houses. "We have thousands of people from other countries living and working on these few streets. Often, they are displaced and illegal, and they live without a union or even a minimum wage. This is one of the richest cities in the world, but in this neighborhood they can't even get clean water. Walk around here in the early morning and you'll see for yourself young girls from all corners making a pilgrimage to the more intact areas of The Quarter, carrying their own clay pots to haul back the day's supply of clean water."

The group paused at what was once a fountain. Its waters were filthy. "Now, it's become a laundry for many of the residents," the guide explained. Indeed, we could have been standing in a third world country.

Lorne and I walked ahead of the others. "Is it really so bad?" I asked him. "Everything that has led to this place?"

"It isn't all bad. It's a marvel, too. And people in general aren't bad." He sighed. "They're just creatures accustomed to pleasure, with a wavering compass. Maybe at one time, people had a better sense of clarity. Which leader was good, which one was evil; which foods were wholesome, and which foods were poison. Now, it's a free for all."

"If that's true, then how come you're the only one who sees it?"

"Every year around Thanksgiving," he said, "my hometown newspaper used to run an article about a turkey that broke free from the pen. There was always one, it seemed. And that turkey was always spared the slaughter."

"Right." The same news story had run in my hometown too. "And people made a big deal of it."

He nodded vigorously. "Like it knew it was doomed and refused to go down without a fight. But it didn't know, of course. Still, the bird was made into a hero." He shrugged. "People see what they want to see."

Walking away after the tour concluded, I could still hear the conviction in Lorne's voice. He understood that humans weren't meant to live on empty. If there was no existential threat, then at least there was antiquing. Or some campaign to save a park. Or golf. Or caring for a purebred puppy that by all of nature's mercy and Darwin's logic should have been extinct, but instead wore booties and ponytails and ate organic lamb treats. In The Quarter it was no different. Maybe it was making tequila, or confections, or baking bread. Or some protest about the labor that went into producing those things. No matter what, there had to be some purpose.

As I left the group behind, I wound my way through the streets, but everything looked unfamiliar in this part of The Quarter. I wandered without thinking through one alley, then another, reaching a still darker part of town. I checked my phone's GPS, but though it showed I was still within The Quarter, it gave nothing more specific.

At one point, I turned down a street that trailed into a wholly unknown neighborhood. Even at night, it was still bustling with plain commerce. People who labored in The Quarter were there, buying groceries for home, or in bulk for the shops where they worked. One plaza was filled with food carts. On a corner, a couple of guys with fiddles played folk music. Vendors called out rhymes to draw customers: *chili mangos sliced, the world's best churros, on my life.*

I stopped at a small cart filled with coconuts. "What's good?" I asked.

"Ah, honey," the man nodded. "Have I got something for you!"

From the depths of his cart he plucked out a coconut, cracked a hole along the top, and then poured in a liberal portion of rum, squeezed in some lime, a pinch of cane sugar, a pinch of ground ginger. He replaced the missing piece of the coconut, shook it vigorously, and then handed it to me. I took it and sipped from a straw, feeling the rum hit me at once.

When I turned the next corner, I saw before me a hulking building still under construction. It took up a vast area between the most commercial parts and the east end where Lorne had led us for the slum tour. The building looked like a tiny Colosseum, and as I drew closer I remembered that I had actually heard about this place. Supposedly, an impulsive investor had erected it during the past year, his vision was to include fighting pits and grand faux matches of wrestling or jousting along with extravagant banquets. Chef Danny Wire had already signed on to the project. It would bring in large crowds—millions of dollars. But then reality hit. The paperwork was pulled, and the construction stalled before completion. Building permits had fallen through without explanation, and now the cavernous construction site lay abandoned.

As I neared, however, I saw it was actually lit up and not empty at all. I entered through an archway, inscribed above with these words: *Bread and Circus*. I ducked past the construction barriers, which had already been pushed aside, and where once there had been a security booth. Inside, a small crowd had gathered, a random assortment of people, mostly men, playing cards in small circles, or cackling over cock fights. Some of the men may have been construction workers who had once worked at the site, those who were the first to know that the project had been abandoned and who now re-purposed it. Most lived and worked in The Quarter. They were the black and brown imports that Lorne had talked about, those who had hungry mouths to feed at home, mouths that waited for them in rooms they shared with two other families. These men were not the exotic beauties showcased in storefronts to personalize pleasure or advertise exclusive authentic experiences. They were the weary ones, the watchful ones, covered in flour with cracked hands after a long day of Making and feeding and grinning for their hipster bosses. They emerged from dank kitchens, rose from the steep staircases in the sidewalk where they spent all day moving boxes. Now at least they could spend a few hours playing games, drinking beer, cracking salty nuts and salty jokes. The half-building had become a refuge where these men, so impotent, so reduced in their foreignness, could feel like men again, at least for a short time.

I was intrigued by this place, but I had no desire to spend time there. So I turned to head back towards the coconut carts and nearly fell over a young girl, pushing her down.

"I'm sorry," I gasped, helping her up. She was pretty, probably Aiden's age, and looking with big eyes that made me think that she, too, had wandered here unknowingly. "Are you okay?"

She smiled apologetically, as if she had been the one to trip me. "Yes, thank you." I couldn't place her accent.

She seemed to be fine. I looked again for the exit but hesitated and then put an arm around her to draw her with me. "Where are you headed? I may get a cab if I can't pick up GPS. Can I drop you home?"

"You are kind." She laughed at the idea. "I'm walking home. It's near."

"You shouldn't be here by yourself. Let me walk with you," I insisted.

"You don't need to."

"I do."

She looked at me as if she were trying to figure out what I wanted from her. At first hesitant, she shrugged and seemed to soften. "I'm Anji." We walked together down several streets of the eastern part of The Quarter, me following her lead. Eventually, she stopped in front of a crumbling building that looked like it was once an old factory plant.

"I'll make sure you get in," I told her. Part of me was curious to see inside her home. She shrugged again and let me in behind her. The door opened onto a narrow vertical corridor of rickety stairs. When we reached the landing, the stairs swung round to another flight. On the top floor, Anji opened a door leading into a hallway.

134

Its yellow paint, once sunny, was now jaundiced.

Anji greeted a couple girls in the hallway then led me to her door, quickly opened it then closed it behind us. "This room is mine."

As soon as I walked inside, I knew I'd made a mistake. Brown brothel stains. Smoke rings blown from the very last cigarette before the apocalypse. A bed sagging at the center. "I didn't realize," I mumbled.

She smiled again, now that her confusion was cleared with my confusion. "You didn't seem to want me."

"How long have you been here?" I asked slowly.

"Two years." Anji spoke carefully, tasting each word for newness or familiarity, like a spoonful from someone else's bowl. I still couldn't place her accent. "My uncle brought me here," she said again and dropped a blanket onto the bed. "Or maybe I was always here..."

She crossed the room and turned on a fan by the widow. It rotated and stirred up the sweet bleached air in the room. It blew the tendrils from Anji's face off round cheeks painted dolly rouge, keen eyes fixed like buttons between them. The thundering emptiness of its spinning blades muffled the moans coming from the other rooms.

"First I cleaned a shop. No dust nowhere." Her face tried to convey the harshness of the demands made of her, darting to seek out the invisible corners of her own room where sinister dust could form, inviting punishment. "They never let me leave, gave me no money. So I ran away. I came here. But," she said with finality, "they kept my papers."

Anji's lips moved reverently over *papers*, like the word was some powerful magic that no mortal could utter without consequence. For a moment, hearing her awe, seeing her head bowed slightly to some greater destiny, I glanced around, half expecting too that it had conjured up some ancient ruthless force that would blow right through the plywood door. But then the fan turned back to us with its ordinary gusts.

"If you had your papers, would you go back home?" I asked.

"No." Anji shook her head shyly, embarrassed for this place, these sheets, and what she had become. She twisted her hair absentmindedly into a thick black coil over one shoulder. Her hair was the stuff of oriental poems—from when people still wrote poems, and still said *oriental*. "Not now. But," she added, almost philosophically, more quietly, "It's okay. I have a plan; I'm waiting for a sign." I looked at her in question. "One day there will be a tall man with yellow hair. Half-human, half-snake. He will find me and that will be the sign. After that, I'll burn down the world."

Was she high? I stood speechless, thinking of this terrifying fantasy from such a sweet-faced girl, probably a warped version of some folklore she'd heard growing up. Abruptly the hallway door opened.

"Micky!" she exclaimed.

He strutted into the room, jutting a thumb at Anji, then at me. "Unless you're on the clock—cash—somebody asked for her."

I bristled, my mothering instincts repelled and furious for her. I wanted to confront him, but Anji held me back with a hand. "It's okay. You don't have to."

Still, I turned to him. "You don't own her, you know."

"Actually, I do." He barely looked at me. "Get out of here."

"Are you threatening me?"

He looked me up and down, assessing me like a seasoned salesman, a bit amused, a bit curious. "What are you?" He shook his head. "Not the law. Not a politician. Not even an activist." He smiled, like that was some inside joke. "No," he decided, with the confidence of a man who trafficked in women's value for a living. "You're nothing."

"I'm not scared of you," I said a bit shaky.

"You should be." His smile did not falter.

Despite trying to put on a brave face, I suddenly felt frightened. "I'm not scared of you," I said again, this time more quietly. I forced myself to calm down, and to feign composure. With some dangerous animals it's best to play dead; with others, better pretend to be dangerous, too. Micky took a step forward. "What do you want?" I asked.

"I want Anji to get back to work. And I want you to know that no one's beyond reach."

With that, he left to tell the man to come along, and after he was gone, Anji said to me, "You should go." Then she whispered even more softly, "Thank you for bringing me home. But don't try to come here again."

"I could bring help. You could tell them."

She shook her head fiercely, as if she would deny whatever I'd said. "Don't bring anyone here. And don't come back."

"It could help."

"No." Her voice was firm, clinging to her delusion. "Remember, I have a plan."

As I turned to go, the client came inside for his turn. He was lean, and poor too, another Quarter dweller. But somehow he had scraped up the money for this. He sat squarely upon the bed. Its springs scraped inside. Anji shuddered, almost imperceptibly, stretching her mouth into the same lavender smile that the other girls had. As I closed the door, she reached out one hand, maybe to me or maybe to the man, and her dress slipped off her shoulder, baring her neck and collarbone.

Suddenly shaken, I raced down the stairs and opened the door to leave, but I had only reached the second floor, and instead of an exit, revealed an open space the size of the entire plant floor. It was filled with girls. In one area, girls who had just come into the city, still thin and bony, were being fattened up, force fed by a matronly woman to drink bowls of lard-filled gruel. In another area, girls who had grown too plump already were being sweated like onions over a heater to melt away the fat. Nearby, other girls were having hairs plucked like feathers, their skins slathered in creams and coconut butter. In other areas girls were being apprenticed in dance, or wine, or tea ceremonies. Nearby, I could even see an old Indian lady on the floor flattening dough with her hands, making chapatti. She had a mud cook stove before her, its primitive clay cracked as if this were a village hut and she was surrounded by a group of girls watching and learning from her so that they could soon go into The Quarter to find jobs making authentic chapatti, too. This floor was a factory grooming girls to be the bodies of The Quarter.

I thought I heard a step on the stairs behind me. Was Micky following? Quickly, I shut the door before me and went flying down the last flight of stairs. Just as I moved to put a hand on the exit door, I saw a nearly dark room off to the other side of the plant, its entrance half-open. I flattened myself to the wall and approached. A couple of teenagers were inside, kids from uptown, not Quarter locals. My eyes adjusted and I saw the room was filled with people splayed on the floor. It seemed to be some kind of hideout, where people, if they paid, could lay low and do who knows what. Maybe they were stoned, maybe they were runaways, or maybe they were just waiting for the next girl upstairs to have fifteen minutes free. Or maybe it was one of those places where they trafficked in hacking and black market phones, untraceable and off the grid, where people could descend into some alternate reality without disruption. Indeed, most of these shadow forms were hunched over phone screens, just as Aiden had been the other morning at breakfast.

Suddenly, I startled. A boy who slouched somewhat near me actually resembled Aiden. I gasped and pulled back so he would not see me. Was it him? I wanted to look but did not dare. What if it was him? Then what? I didn't know. Shaking, I threw open the plant door and ran outside.

A short distance away, I checked GPS again but still couldn't get a precise location. This part of The Quarter was totally unfamiliar. I tried to retrace my steps but found myself at a dead end. A group of children sat playing. "How do I get to the main part of The Quarter?" I called out.

Hearing me, they delighted, and as a body rose up and raced toward me, chattering and grinning. They spoke in many different languages, but they seemed to have a single language, too, in which they could all communicate with each other—a universal children's language of common items like sticks and balls and coins and sweets. I seemed to hear mimicry of my request. "The Quarter?" one asked from behind. "The Quarter... The Quarter... The Quarter..."

From every side they swarmed round me, pulling at my clothes, picking at my pockets. It felt like they might overwhelm and consume me. I tried to avoid them, these frail feathery children, but like a swarm of insects, they were too many, too mighty.

So I pushed them off in one great heave and started to run as I had never run before, driven by adrenaline, navigating by some instinct toward an area of sky where, bleached by the lights below, there seemed to be no stars. Running, I found myself using muscles that had grown soft and milky over the years but suddenly, in my fear, had new fight or flight purpose and super human strength. Even when I burst into Paris, nearly knocking over a portrait artist as he painted a middle-aged couple in just-purchased berets, I continued to run. Soon I heard nothing but my breath and heart and the pounding of my feet until they found a rhythm together and eventually the plant and the children and The Quarter all fell behind. When I finally stopped running, I broke down and cried.

14.

I woke the next morning after the standoff with Micky and lay in bed, still shaken. Turning into the down comforter, it puffed against my cheek, like a squashy merengue. What impossible softness. What billowy surrender. What astounding privilege, to wake in the midst of such luxury, like milk-skinned royalty, while a couple of miles away, Anji lived a very different life.

Of all the people in the world, why should I be so lucky? It was a gloomy thought. I sat up to shake it off and went to make coffee. I bustled around the kitchen and then set the table with a bowl of cereal, milk, and berries, and some tea in a chipped teacup. I plucked a blueberry from the bowl and tasted it. It was one of those fat fresh ones, nickel-sized and bursting its skin, almost violet in color and tasting like the grass and mint leaves that had shared the same patch of earth: a *perfect* berry.

There were so many people in the world with little food or no meal at all this morning. The homeless man in our neighborhood certainly needed more than he had. What gave *me* the right to such a berry? What gave me the right to anything?

In everything I did that morning, I compared myself to Anji, or to people in some other part of the world, or some other class or fortune. Every thought I formed, every action, even the fluidity of free choice that I unthinkingly exercised were all defined by privilege.

I got dressed and walked to the corner store where I bought a copy of every newspaper and magazine there. I spent most of the day on the couch, poring over the news articles, looking for the *other* reality—perhaps the true reality—seeking out people without quiet houses, without blankets, and without blueberries.

Aiden came home from the gym as I was reading a story about women in the Congo who were raped and broken and so mutilated that they would never again take a proper piss. They leaked wherever they went and stank so people sometimes threw them out of the village and left them for the wild animals to eat.

"Call it research, if you want. But you know what this looks like, right?" Aiden had been watching me for a while as he stretched. Again, I saw a glimpse of that figure in the dark room in the old plant. He looked at the square pile of newspapers before me, limp from refolding and highlighting. His tank-top was soaked in a dark sickle shape after basketball. He took a Gatorade from the refrigerator and cracked it open, chugging a quarter of the blue bottle in a single gulp. "You're a rubbernecker."

And he was right, of course. Jack had called me on it, too, my voyeurism. Whenever I felt lost, my head would envision or seek out contrasts and desperation, driven by some clannish need to know my own hearth, my destiny, as opposed to others. To Jack, always practical and accustomed to instant gratification, such counterfactual thinking was one of my most puzzling qualities: the need to say, I am this caste, not that caste. Maybe Aiden had inherited his critical eye for this from him.

After that, I did my reading locked inside my bedroom, trying somehow to find those other people and fill myself with their lives, and their grimness. I read essays by doctors who spent years amputating limbs in Syria, marveling that the stories were written afterwards, as they sat in pleasant coffee shops, somehow having moved past the horror. I memorized statistics and read sections out loud. I pondered: was it better for atrocity to be visible, or did that only normalize it? Was it better for a slave to be miserable in slavery, or to know nothing else, to have no vocabulary or context or self-awareness?

Moving away from the here and now, I found myself thinking about beheadings and crucifixions. Maybe it was a sudden fall into depression. Maybe it was a way of understanding the torture, or of weighing the relative easiness and luxury in which I walked the earth. That night, when I got into bed, I wrapped myself in my blankets, spent and empty. Something in the horror of each story read, the faux immediacy of commonplace cruelty, became like a near-death experience from which nothing ever looks the same again. Each moment made me stretch into the absurdities of privilege: How to squander my talent? How to waste my days? How, from my place of comfort, to make peace with the underlying cruelty and apathy of humankind?

Had there ever been a time when whole civilizations were sweepingly moved to goodness, maybe by shofar calls or haunting hymns in a cavernous cathedral or promises of grace? Maybe, but there had been far more ugliness for sure. I tried to recall acts of goodness I'd seen, even of individuals, but they fell short.

The week before at Channing, Ruth moderated a panel event on a recent genocide. Afterward, as I helped her clean up, I saw a rich donor, moved and even humbled by it all. He came up to her at the podium, fat fingers fumbling as he wrote a big check. It was some extension of his usual self-importance, as if to say, I can't do it, but someone somewhere, scrubbed clean and earnest and Christian, can drive the ambulance, clean the pus, live poor on my behalf. Was that goodness? Maybe…

Mostly, there were moments of a special kind of cruelty from people who either have always had power or have been at the mercy of it. It became clear to me in bed: people live blithely, unthinkingly in their circumstance, at times jealous, at times moved to something bigger. But humanity's reflection on injustice or tragedy, its attempt at empathy is usually not much greater than the horror of one's nearness to it: that someone else's tragedy is so close that it could have been mine.

When I finally fell asleep, I dreamed of the stories I'd read: sex slaves; gangs burying people alive; entire towns devastated by hurricanes and floods and left to rot. Shipments of condoms hijacked by religious groups and set on fire. An exposé in the *Christian Science Monitor*: A low table in the hut was spread with a cloth. The women lay the young girl upon it and moved her clothes aside so that she was bare. Her mother was the one who held her legs down and open. And then, swiftly, the old woman took a razor blade and cut her, sprinkling powder and pressing a rag to the blood in one motion. 'You'll be just the same again soon,' they said. As if that could be.

I sat up in bed, shaken, and then, eventually, talked myself back into a fitful sleep. Soon I was dreaming again. This time it was the *Time* story about two women in a market on the other side of the world. They were shopping for scarves. One chose a square scarf with large dots in plum, cherry, and orange. Her friend chose a long olive scarf that wrapped around her neck several times. They walked home admiring the scarves, draping them over themselves, twisting them into skirts, coiling the sleeves, touching the cool silk to each other's cheeks, laughing and talking. Then they turned the corner, and there was a man wearing his own scarf wrapped round his face. And he threw acid at them. They shrieked to God, and they pulled each other away from the man and toward the grocery on the corner. By the time they reached the store the man was gone. "Help!" they begged, writhing. "Water!" The grocer brought all the water he had. Then the woman who sold shoes next door brought jugs from her shop, too. But still they burned.

These twisted realities hissed and leaked from my dreams like a poisonous gas, seared through the pleasant streets of my neighborhood, then circled round and drifted back to me, dulling me more till they made sense on some level in my sleep: the universe would punish anyone disturbing its order.

———————

After my encounter with the mean underbelly of The Quarter, and weary from all the nightmares, I resolved to only ever go to the safe and mainstream spots there. I wanted to forget about what happened that day.

At times though, I could not help myself, I thought again of Anji, what it would take to track her down again, to sit in the back of a police car and direct them through all those streets, in the ease of daylight and their safety, past the Colosseum, to the old plant, up those dank stairs, and finally to bust into her room and save her. But then I remembered her face as she told me never to return. It was hard to fathom, but she was loyal to her fantasy, her plan, and to the man who rented her that room.

Anji remained in my mind even as I tried desperately to push away thoughts of her. I threw myself into my work instead, focusing on Penny, and her poetry project. The busyness on campus was exactly what I needed.

When Philip came back in town, we went out together more often, sampling all the hot new restaurants. We had dinner on a yacht one night with a group of his friends. As the water moved in majestic black slips around us, I couldn't help but wonder what Sawyer might think of being onboard a gold crested yacht? Whatever my hesitation might have been, we all got into the hot tub and took bowls of oysters to eat and Moscow Mules to drink, and soon that smaller circle of water bubbling massage jets in the boat seemed more significant than the larger one lapping outside of it.

One night, I told Aiden about a restaurant that Philip and I had passed in The Quarter. "It's called the Doll House, but they say it has all kinds of toys." I shrugged. "Should we go tomorrow? It's supposed to be fun for families."

As soon as I said *families,* I wanted to bite back the word. Aiden's face seemed to crack open, exposing all the hurt he held inside. "I'm with Dad tomorrow. So that won't work." He paused. "Unless you think we should all go?"

I saw he was expecting me to say no, bracing himself for it. And with a deep pang, I thought, what if I could give him this small gift, to have both his parents in the same room, for the same meal? We had not done such a thing since the divorce, only meeting in passing at pickup and drop-off points. But perhaps, for Aiden, we could bring ourselves to do it. It would be awkward, of course. But I had started to move on, and maybe this was the next step.

"Okay," I said. "Let's all go."

So the next night we three sat down together, and in some ways it felt the same as it always had felt, our separate energies now merged, looking over the menu in anticipation. But the Doll House itself had a strangeness that soon settled upon us.

I'd expected the restaurant to have everything in miniature. I imagined the food prepared with tweezers and nail scissors, served on doll-house sized china plates and cups, delivered to us via toy trains. We would eat with cocktail forks from tiny scoops and squares that were not filling but tasty and with so many courses so at least we would not leave hungry.

But actually, in the Doll House, instead of everything being shrunken, the toys and the world they occupied were blown up. When we entered the dining room it felt like we were actually in the dining room of a doll-house. And just like in a doll-house, many of the details were not real but actually painted onto the paisley walls: the windows and the meadow view beyond and the curtains gathered on either side were all illustrations on the wallpaper, and even some of the furniture around the room was painted on the wallpaper, with a cozy looking armchair and an old-fashioned bureau displaying ceramic shepherdesses, all flat but approximating reality.

In the center of the room, were spread round tables where people sat, drinking cocoa and eating cupcakes, or having dinner like us off enormous flat dishes. But it was not just the three of us at the table. Instead, each table had its own life-sized dolls seated around it, frozen in a plastic pose. The table next to us had a tall Barbie holding court, blonde and buxom and peach; a table in the corner had a superhero spaceman, faceless behind his helmet. Our table had a Raggedy Ann doll that was taller than me, grinning and gripping a rubber apple.

The obtuseness of the place, with its retro and ironic touches, made perfect sense in The Quarter. But sitting there with our family together again in a bit of our old wholesomeness, it seemed wrong, and we were quietly uncomfortable.

I turned to Jack, trying to be breezy. "Have you been to any other Quarter joints lately?" By joints I meant restaurants, of course. And Jack started to talk about a Thai place that he had gone to when his mother was in town. But as I said the word joints, it seemed to me that Aiden turned red suddenly, and it was quite a few minutes before he made eye contact again. Was that really Aiden there that night? I wondered again, as I had already wondered many times since then. It certainly had looked like him. Was the old plant the place he thought about when I said the word *joint*?

I studied Aiden's face. Often he was unreadable. After seeing others with multiple children, it sometimes seemed it was almost easier the more you had, as you could always read a child in relation to the others and know where they stood. Jack's sister had three. Her oldest child, Lillianna, always saw herself at the center of any question. Her second child always saw himself reflected off his older sister—forever keen to contradiction. Her third child was usually off in some frontier or no-man's land, chiseling out a new position for himself.

Aiden, as our one and only child, and without the counterpoints, usually was a puzzle. This day, though, I believed I could read him plainly and felt almost certain that he was thinking about the old plant, and that we were both remembering that dank place full of terrible rooms.

Even if it was not him, did it make a difference? It was another boy just like him, so in some ways, it was only a matter of time till he made his way there or somewhere else like it.

Gulping in horror, I picked up my teacup, big as a bowl, and I had a moment of clarity, a premonition: in The Quarter, Aiden was doomed, I was doomed, we all were doomed.

"What?" Jack's banter on the Thai place subsided. "What now?" He could read the darkness on my face, like second nature. He knew where my mind always went, ill at ease and suspicious, taking years off our life together for no reason, when all he wanted to do was be in the here and now and order an appetizer already. Since the divorce his tone was even less tolerant with it. "It's always something heavy, isn't it? We're always just one domino flick away from calamity. I tell you," he folded his lips tersely, "this is not one of the things I miss. Sorry, kiddo," he frowned at Aiden with real regret, "not much I can do for you now."

The two exchanged a knowing look, and I saw another of the many moments in which it was clear that Aiden was more Jack's child than mine.

I sat quiet in answer.

"Awkward." Aiden grimaced.

"Anyway." Jack cleared his throat to reboot. "How do you like teaching?"

I forced myself to shake off the last moments. We were all there for a reason, weren't we? I needed to focus. "It's actually great," I told him sincerely. "It's changed everything."

He softened at my enthusiasm. "I think it's wonderful that you're doing it. I'm sure you're great, Talia." He looked at me with such genuine warmth, rooting for me, feeling some pride in me. Even after everything, we would always be intertwined. "You so loved subbing for your dad. In fact, I'm pretty sure you were hoping he'd have another bout of mono the following semester."

I cracked a small smile. "I wouldn't put that past me." If I had been like this always, if *we* had been like this always, maybe the marriage would have lasted.

I took a deep breath, kept my eyes on my baby boy, my plate, then back to my baby boy. Putting all my fears for Aiden aside, I focused instead on this one tangible thing before me instead—making his family as whole as it could be, talking to Jack, carving out some new normalcy. I realized we were not all good yet, Jack and I, but we were getting there. We had to get there.

15.

Final exams came and went, first with self-important student panic, everyone needing something immediately, and then just as quickly, when it was all done, with everyone eager to be far gone and not look back. All that remained was Penny's thesis presentation and defense.

As I walked across the quad, watching students pack the contents of their dorm rooms into their cars, I breathed in the crisp smell of snow soon to come, the scent that makes the body want hot drinks and hibernation. Suddenly, I thought of Sawyer again, but just as quickly I put him out of my mind.

I doubled back to the Humanities hall and joined several other professors in the Hearth room. Ruth was there, and Sebastian too, and a few others that I had only met in passing. We sat around a long wooden table with our coffee mugs and the carefully collated copies of *Stiletters* that Penny had placed at each chair.

"I also made cupcakes," she announced coming in from the side door, carrying a platter that looked like a display of tall stiletto stripper shoes. Each had a fluffy cupcake as the ball of the foot and then an ice cream cone fused with fondant for the length of the shoe and another cone for the high heel. She passed around the platter, every shoe a different combination of orange and pink and purple with a dusting of emerald sugar. I chose one and took a bite and smiled at Penny.

After everyone was seated, Penny walked to the front of the table to recite a selection of her poems. She planted two hands on the back of the empty chair at the head of the table and looked at each of us, one by one. "Hurt me," she began. One or two of the others gasped. All of us sat at attention. "Hurt me with your eyes.

Hurt me with your hands. Hurt me with your dollar bills, hurt me on demand." Penny twisted as she spoke so the recitation became almost a lap dance. "With your laws, with your claws, with your perceptions of my flaws." She put one heeled leg up on a chair, ran a hand slowly down the length of her body, then smacked the hand down again on the table. "Till I want it, till I've spawned it, till I'm bloody and I'm daunted." She bent over to the side, throwing the top of her body forward, letting her hair tumble over in a splash. Slowly, she rolled up once more, her back arching like calligraphy, performing till the poem was done. "Hurt me."

It was grotesque, but with some brief moments of gorgeousness. Next, she read a poem about being a puppeteer, pulling at strings that controlled the men in the strip club. Then a poem about being old and musing what it would be like years later to go back through the boxes of stilettos and glittery pasties. Then a poem from the point of view of the stripper's pole, and another as a bottle of vodka. She finished with an ode to her boyfriend Donald—and to his wife. In each poem, she seemed to be charged and in command of the experience. There was a startling magnetism in the force of her exhibitionism. I recognized it, because I once wrote like that, too.

When she had finished the reading segment, she left the room so the faculty could discuss her work in private before she returned for the defense. The room was quiet as she closed the door behind her.

"Well," Ruth burst out first. She drew her long wool sweater around her and beamed. "As a feminist response to the patriarchy, this has turned out to be a project of real excellence." Immediately, the others began to weigh in, speaking to the group at large, to each other and over each other, all congratulating the work and Penny on its boldness. Each tried to sound important.

Having never been on this side of a defense committee before, I determined to sit back and observe at the start. I saw each professor eager for his say, anxious to bring the lens of their discipline to the forefront, to somehow claim Penny's work for his department. As it went on, I found myself cringing in my chair, unable to stop watching the professors and the conviction of their dialogue. I saw that the way each professor gave support or deference or pushback, and to whom, was actually part of a much larger tapestry. Here was academia at its worst, with all its preposterous hierarchies and political pecking orders that reeked of feudalism.

Now as the group of professors debated and digressed, all seemed to be saying the same thing: Penny's work was a success, but it was a credit to Women's Studies—no, to the English Department—no, to Sociology. Were they applying for funding? I wondered: Was there some quota system I didn't know about? I couldn't imagine what was fueling this smallness. Maybe they'd been uncomfortable with her poetry pushing the edge, so they were over-compensating with this enthusiasm; Sebastian *had* been a mortified purple during the entire first poem. Maybe it just happened to be a perfect storm of people needing to prove themselves—one a new Chair, one up for tenure, and so on.

Or maybe it was indeed as they had always said: Academic politics were the most bitter, because the stakes were so low.

"That's just how it works," Philip once explained to me. "The system *needs* professors fighting over nothing, debating the proper annotation in a journal article or vying to teach a class for two or three thousand dollars and no benefits. That way they can really invest in the new gymnasiums that bring the college prestige and the more pampered clients—I mean students." He paused. "A degree is now just a product, really."

I thought of this now as I watched the show before me, of bickering academics trying to seem valuable in this place where there was no rhyme or reason to value anymore. Finally, I couldn't take it.

"Hold up," I interrupted loudly. "Don't we have any questions for Penny?" Everyone was quiet. "I mean, it was a captivating performance, but there was plenty of cliché too. And isn't she supposed to defend her work? And aren't we supposed to ask questions?" They looked at me blankly. "Such as why she chose this genre? Or why each poem is hitting the same exact note? And where's the nuance?"

"You're going to ask a victim about nuance?" Ruth and some of the others looked at me like I was crazy. "Remember my article on child brides last year?" she asked the group. "It was in *The Chron-icle*," she reminded them pointedly, as if she hadn't told them all before. "It illustrated how victims are simply victims across the spec-trum—strippers or raped or cat-called or child brides—whatever. To seek gradations, to question the context or relativity or nuance, would be to victimize her again." She recited this last part as an ad-monishment, speaking plainly to me, as if I were a child.

"You don't understand nuance," I muttered, pressing my lips to-gether. "Or victims."

I had seen victims up close. I had seen Anji. And even as a victim, she nurtured some defiant fantasy wrapped up in her own pride. Her delusion of unleashing an apocalypse someday when she got some mythical sign from some mythical yellow-haired giant, half-man, half-snake—it was something she had probably heard in a fairytale or a film. But she'd clung to it for years, turning it into her daily salvation. Who knows how Anji pictured the world after it had gone down in flames? Whatever that looked like, I suspected, Anji imagined it often, licking her lips, transporting herself away from her shabby room, and whatever man was on top of her at the time— and often, the rebellion of this fantasy was more real and important to her than any other tangible, miserable aspect of her victim's life.

I had seen other victims too. I had seen my grandmother who was literally a slave for years under the Nazis. Eventually, she lost her husband, and raised her child alone. During her last years when we lived with her, I realized, she had never really managed to emerge from that hell. She would be on the farm or at the beach for a barbe-cue and still I saw her fingering the tattooed numbers on her arm, a gesture which started in the early days in anguish, evolved over time to become a nervous habit, and in her last years settled into a kind of meditation, a ritual she performed while gathering her thoughts.

But I could also see my grandmother on one of her good days when we lived there. She took me out to milk the cows with her, kind of manic, trying to trick the good energy into entering her dying body by using it with abandon, as if it were nothing, and at the same time endless.

Afterward, she brought me back, the sloshing pail in hand, the closest she had ever been to gleeful. "Drink the milk straight," she said. "Especially the cream, it's the best part." I drank deeply and she took pleasure from the pleasure on my face. "Isn't it splendid? Isn't it all splendid?" She threw one arm out to the farm and the country that spread in every direction all the way to Jerusalem. But even her pleasures were heavy. "Your grandfather never came here. But there is soul everywhere in this place. His soul, too." She thought about my grandfather all the time. She heard him whistling till the day she died.

That was her victim's legacy—still tattooed and haunted, but delighted too by a drink of cream and the whistle of a song from a lifetime before. How could I have ever defined her without nuance, without context?

And hadn't I thought of myself as a victim too? For the first time in a long while, as I listened to the faculty discussion wind round me, I thought of how I, too, had foolishly felt a victim for years, a prisoner in our own house. I pictured Aiden, not as he was today, but as he had been when he was younger and malleable and *mine*. When I knew the details of his face in a primal way, as only a mother can: every freckle, the mischievous smile, the pout set to erupt, the keen look of learning, each word uttered to say one thing though something else is actually meant and only I knew it. And somehow in those years, every day benevolently full of intimacy and minutia and so much time with Aiden, this wondrous love of my life—who would one day be beyond reach—somehow I also felt trapped. The fortune of that time and that trap were at once both truths. And so, really, there was nothing without nuance.

With Ruth's thesis on child brides spelled out, the room of professors was ready to move on. But I wasn't. "I think I'll just ask her a question or two when she comes back. It will only take a minute." Everyone turned to me with stony eyes, like this last bit had crossed a line. "What? She chose to strip. She chose to put these stories out into the public. Surely she'll be okay discussing them respectfully, even if there are conflicting views. If we don't do that, I think we're selling her short."

"This is just aggressive." The room broke into a loud buzz. They all had expected a particular dialogue with an agreed-upon premise and rules of relativity: us versus them, this is good, that is bad. And if someone happened to come from another point of view, well, they expected they would with sound reasoning see their error, welcome the deliverance, and leave enlightened. No one knew what to do with it when suddenly they saw there was someone in their midst—a woman, no less, and brown to boot—who came with the exact opposite context and purpose, but equally passionate and reasoned out. The whole construct was thrown off entirely and everyone was in an uproar so that even I started to doubt myself. Maybe I didn't understand progress after all, and had gone so far in one direction that I'd actually circled back around to the other side of the pendulum? Suddenly, we found ourselves in a booby-trapped chess game, where no one knew what trumped what—brown pieces or white pieces, this queen or that queen—and there was no such thing as checkmate.

"Enough," Sebastian banged one hammy hand on the table, quieting the room again. He glared at me. "We will not be questioning the victim here. The last thing we need is anyone doubting the politically correct sensibilities of this institution. This is a safe space and there will be no triggers under my watch."

When Penny returned, she still wore the boldness of her performance. But she gave a quick glance over her shoulder, a nervous search, to see how she had been received, and I understood that she was just a girl after all, trying to weigh in on things she did not yet grasp, and to affect the world. And I had failed her somehow—we all had—because she had emerged from college with nothing. She was, at the end of her learning, perfectly unchanged.

Ruth had her sit at the head of the table. "Thank you, Penny." She looked deeply into her eyes. "We honor your experience. And this beautiful project." Penny sighed in relief as she heard this. In that moment, any inclination to critique and her own self-reflection dissipated. She was hapless Penny again, soothed and gratified, believing that the simple act of creation made her work right and complete. There was a de facto validity in its very existence. "This work is exactly what it's supposed to be."

Chairs scraped backward as professors nodded and exclaimed and congratulated and came to her with hugs. Her thesis would pass with the highest marks. As we went through the motions, signing the paperwork, ushering her toward an empty degree, I felt a numb bewilderment, that this couldn't possibly be real. But, after all, it was.

16.

That night I called Sawyer. The day had been such a failure, and Philip was already on a plane and couldn't stop me, so I picked up the phone and dialed.

"I'm sorry. I was a complete idiot," he said before I could say anything.

"I was an idiot, too."

Without hesitation he told me, "I'm coming over." When he arrived he rushed inside, drawing me to him at once. "I've missed you," he whispered.

I pressed myself to him, and in that moment we were alive again. We tumbled toward my room and fell into bed, not artfully like in the movies, rather tripping over the edge of the hallway rug. But it didn't make a difference. And with him beside me in bed it felt so natural. Afterward, we fell asleep together only to wake again in the middle of the night, reaching for each other.

Out of the blue, Lena called the next morning. The phone woke me as Sawyer slept nearby. Since I hadn't heard from her in weeks, despite all my messages, I almost didn't answer. I just listened to its trill, but at the last minute I picked up. "What?"

"I want you to preview the hall of sweets today," she said at once.

"Where have you been?" I asked, still groggy but irritated that after her long absence she just expected that I would be available. Before her radio silence, I had begun to think that we were actually becoming friends. I felt hurt by her sudden disappearance.

"Oh, no, are you pissed at me? Is it because I didn't call?" She seemed a bit put out to be discussing ordinary life such as answering phone calls and returning messages. "Is that what people do?" she sighed. "I meant to call you. It's been so hectic here."

"Well, that's something." I muttered. "A start, anyway."

"Good," she rushed on. "The truth is that I need you—your input. You're kind of my target market for this hall, so you're the perfect guinea pig. And you can bring Sawyer, too," she offered grudgingly when I didn't jump at her offer. "If you want to, I mean."

"I don't know if that's going to work," I said softly, watching him stir. How would he feel about going there again?

"What?" She turned sullen. "I've had you guys here as much as I could. You owe me."

"Look, I'll have to run it by him," I hedged.

"It's the *hall of sweets*," Lena said crisply. "Do you have any idea what that means? Beyond anything you can imagine!"

I felt intrigued. I'd been trying to get back to Prongs, and here was my chance. "We'll probably be there," I told her as I hung up. Sawyer turned over to face me.

"What? Where are we going?"

"This is so nice." I ran a hand over his cheek. "And I don't want to mess it up. But," I said to him, putting my head on his chest, "we're invited to Prongs again."

"Prongs is a bit too crazy for me," Sawyer said carefully, also not wanting to ruin our reunion.

"Give it one more chance," I said instead. "Lena just called. This room will be different. It's not even up and running yet. Plus, it's *sweets*." He looked doubtful. "Do you have any clue what the wait is to get into Prongs? Up to a year for some rooms. Not to mention the cost," I informed him primly. "We've been able to come and go as we like. How lucky are we?"

"Okay. Okay." He looked at me and I tried to let myself sink into his gaze. "But no more getting lucky for a while." He slid his hands down my back. "Not like that, anyway. You know the rule, right? You're only allowed one spell of crazy per relationship."

"Okay," I promised. "Then this is it."

———

That evening, Sawyer and I walked all the way to Prongs in the comfortable quiet that had so easily resumed between us. As the steps passed, we found our gait together. Jack was so tall that through all the years we never had a good gait. His arm would wrap over my shoulder heavily. And he had a longer step so we always bumped into one another. But Sawyer had one arm down my back and around my waist and I fit there naturally, step for step, with my handbag swinging off my other wrist.

Lena led us through one of the smaller hallways in the main Prongs cavern, turning off onto another hallway, and then another. "We've only been developing this room recently," she explained. "But it's more or less finished now and we've officially started taking reservations for next week." She stopped at the last door at the end of the corridor. "Which means you have it all to yourselves tonight," she announced with a noble sweep of her arm, throwing open the door to a grand circular room.

The space was not so big but it stretched two stories high. Every wall, up to the very top, was lined with shelves, and the shelves were stocked with candy jars and books, books and candy jars, broken up only by ladders on wheels clinging to one level or another. The floor of the room itself was a maze of reading nooks, and at each were stacks of more books and candy jars.

"It's a library," I gasped. "A library of candy." Even Sawyer was amazed.

Lena laughed. "I figured you would appreciate this place."

"Where does one even start?" Sawyer asked her.

"Well, you can just eat and read, of course, and make your way through the labyrinth. Fairy tales, myths, poetry, plays, classics in every language. Ancient manuscripts that were long ago stolen or hidden in some monastery library, manuscripts that many believe never even existed. They're all here, classified by section. Or," she paused dramatically. "You can play the game. See, each candy jar holds some confection inspired by a book. A sugar drop or gumball, some square of Turkish delight or stretch of toffee. The jar gives you a clue to the book that inspired it. If you can track it down, voila, the perfect pairing!"

When we didn't move, Lena laughed delightedly and stepped up onto one of the ladders. "We could begin here." She gave an elegant swish of her leg, like an ice-skater, and sent the ladder rolling toward the middle of a shelf, scooting around the arc of the room.

"Or here!" she called out at random as she pulled a tall glass jar off the shelf. She opened it and gave each of us a bright magenta drop, soft and dusted with flecks of gold.

I put it carefully into my mouth. It was infused with rose oil and herbs. "It's delicious. Flowery, sort of green," I suggested. "But I have no idea what to do with that," I confessed.

Sawyer sucked on his sweetmeat, content in waiting to see where this would go. Lena tasted hers carefully, and then nodded. Checking the inside of the jar cover, she read the inscription. "Here's your clue!"

She handed me the jar lid. I read it carefully. "...Stolen the impression of her fantasy with bracelets of thy hair, rings, gawds, conceits, knacks, trifles, nosegays, sweetmeats..."

I broke into a grin. I knew it immediately. "Shakespeare." I held up the jar and peered at the sweetmeats that remained. "But it's the fairy dust that gives it away." I confidently placed the lid back on the jar. "*A Midsummer Night's Dream*," I announced.

Lena finished her last bite and closed her eyes. Balanced on the rung of the ladder, she held out her arms. "Do you feel that?"

"I feel like I can fly," Sawyer agreed.

I too held out my arms, sensing the lift. "Maybe I will."

Lena caught herself gracefully, as if she too had been about to leap from the ladder. She gave another sweep of her leg, reaching the end of one shelf, and then hopped upon the ladder of the next shelf, rolling forward to very nearly the end of that one, too. Sawyer and I hurried after her to the Shakespeare section. The row of books before her was striped in gilded volumes and faint edges that smelled of old ink and old paper. She moved along it with one finger, then stopped and retrieved a very ancient looking copy of *A Midsummer*

Night's Dream. "An early printing..." She handed it to me and I took it reverently. "I'm sure I don't have to tell *you* to be careful."

I held the candy jar in one hand and the book in the other as Lena hopped off the ladder and started to work her way back to the door. "You can just sit with those if you want. Read and nibble. Or," she told us, "you can play."

After she left, Sawyer and I barely glanced at each other, and then just took off in separate directions. He said something about looking at a stack of old pages of sheet music from the 1500s. Meanwhile, I raced around collecting rare early editions of *David Copperfield* and *Ivanhoe.* I stopped to eat a candy-like cake soaked in alcohol and topped with a cherry. The label on the jar read: "When a true genius appears in the world, you may know him by this sign, that the dunces are all in confederacy against him." And I laughed and laughed to myself, thinking of my beloved Ignatius J. Reilly, grotesque, in his floppy hunting cap, bellowing and eating these very cakes.

I sat down with the books I'd collected in an enormous leathery armchair. The coffee table in front of it had several illuminated manuscripts upon it, and a large glass jar of what tasted like jellied wine drops.

I had to laugh at myself, because of all the decadent pleasures at Prongs, the one that so far thrilled me the most was eating candy drops and cautiously, ever so cautiously, leafing through those brittle book pages.

Each wine drop was delicious, so I kept eating them, but I was too absorbed by the books to count. Who can say how many I had eaten before I noticed JB Picard sitting in an armchair nearby. He was eating a loop of taffy and leafing through a book. I blinked, and he was gone.

Suddenly, everything felt wrong.

I looked at the label on the wine drops. "Among us Cyclopes the fertile earth produced rich grape clusters, and Zeus' rain swells them: but this is a taste from a stream of ambrosia and nectar." My breath quickened and I stood up clumsily. Where was Sawyer? I stumbled forward to look for him. I ducked behind an enormous mahogany desk and followed a path between two rows of low shelves. They were spread with ancient medical drawings, the bodies looking splayed open, their organs and intestines like creatures in their own right. I followed the corridor of shelves but it led into a dead-end corner of glass jars, jellied snakes that seemed to be writhing, jellied embryos turning and growing from moment to moment, and then many more jars of candied insects teeming over each other, marzipan mice that scratched at the glass, spiders coated in syrup, beetles crusty from sugar seething in their terrible living pile.

Horrified, I turned to go. But my movements were rippled and clumsy and my hand swept around me in a purple haze, knocking the jar of beetles to the floor. I saw the jar crack in slow motion, one clean break across its middle, and then they came pouring out, hissing and crawling over me, into my clothes, into my ears and mouth. Brushing the beetles from me as best I could, I backed out of that corner and ran through the labyrinth. "Sawyer!" I heard no answer. "Sawyer!" I called again, my voice catching.

I saw an exit door and opened it. Could he have left? The silver corridor outside was empty, but maybe from the corner of my eye, I saw a shadow of movement, of form, turning the corner to the right. I slid out and ran down the hallway.

Pausing to catch my breath, I leaned against a door. Its silver chains felt solid and bumpy along my spine. From somewhere deep inside the room, I heard a terrible moan. A chill crawled under my skin. I pressed my ear to the door but did not hear it again.

"It's nothing," I whispered, trying to stay calm.

I looked more closely at the door. A shape emerged on the surface, an ancient etching in bronze over the silver chain behind it. It revealed a great cow standing over a raging fire. It's just a barbecue, I told myself. Just a door. Just a room.

I heard the sound again, this time clearly a moan of pain. "Stop," I whispered to myself. "Stop making up horror stories."

I looked again at the animal on the door. Then I noticed the horns. It was not a cow, it was a bull. Square lines on one side of its body revealed a door leading into the figure's interior. Stories of Greek torture, Romans roasting saints alive; and then from the room another moan, an ancient sound that had once horrified civilizations but perhaps had not been heard again for many centuries—not until this time in this place. Trapped human screams emerged as the bellow of a brazen bull.

It's not real, I told myself. Those sick ironic freaks.

I forced myself to breathe deeply, to notice the rise and fall of my chest. Suddenly, I saw that the shadowy line down the hallway was actually broken, and the place from where the shadow emanated was a room with its door cracked open. I tiptoed closer. Peering through the crack, I saw an ordinary locker room.

The guy on the bench looked familiar. He took out a can of hairspray as he teased his hair into wild knots. "If I stay with this gig, I'm going to have to move uptown."

Another guy stood near him, closer to the door, leaning impatiently against the wall. "Finish up already. I need help. The entire zoo is on the run here tonight."

I turned and raced back toward the library. As I edged around the corner of the hallway, I stopped short. Ten paces away a man came toward me, stumbling and demonic, probably fuzzy from sedatives. He was shirtless and I saw the brown flesh of his back and chest were covered in raw uniform scars of strips, like bacon. I screamed silently and fumbled backward. I should help him, I thought. He clearly needed help, his flesh shredded and salt-cured by some French-trained chef for a sum of money, that would be sent back home to family. I heard again what Sawyer had said to me—it seemed so long ago now—about what a terrible thing free-choice bacon would be.

I should help him, I thought again, but the jellied beetles seemed to crawl underneath my clothing. I couldn't clear my head enough to do anything, and somehow I knew if I stopped, I would never get out of this place. I started to feel my way back down the hallway, and let the man go his way.

There was the library! Throwing open the door, I slammed it again behind me in relief. "Sawyer," I said hoarsely, searching the stacks again. "Sawyer!" I nearly screamed.

"Where are you?" he called from somewhere within the stacks.

Finding myself in another dark corner, I cried, "Sawyer, I'm here." I needed to be near him, to kiss him and let him envelop me. Clawing at the insects swarming my body again, I caught a glimpse of him through a circle of couches. I raced forward, but as I neared, his form looked somehow different. He was not vulnerable in his usual way. I drew up short.

Sawyer's ordinary features suddenly showed ugly lines, like a mug shot in a newspaper story. He was licking his chops and the torso of his body seemed hulking and bumpy. Goosebumps formed along my arms and a hunt or be hunted energy pushed through my veins. Frightened and angry, I knew there was only one thing I could do.

I threw myself at him, my mouth one minute at his cheek, as if in a kiss, and then I was biting through skin and flesh. Everywhere the room bled purple, and he was trying to pull me off of him, but I clung to him with my arms and my teeth clamped. When he managed to push me away, I leapt back and clawed at his neck and shoulder, loosing flesh and blood and skin and more purple.

The purple only faded when I heard Lena's voice. "You crazy bitch…"

And then I remember cold water splashing on my face and someone shaking me and some pill pushed down my throat. Later I woke in a perfectly white room, on a perfectly white velvet couch, my cheek on a white cushion with only a death march of seam stitched down it. I sat up, everything suddenly horribly clear again now, with the aching muscles of my jaw and the taste of Sawyer's flesh still caught in my teeth.

17.

I bolted up from the couch and tried to open the door. It was locked. I looked around the room for another exit. Then I noticed my mouth again, swollen and tasting of gauze. The details of the attack came back in a rush. I hunted this way and that and spotted the narrow bathroom door off to one side. Fleeing toward it, I bumped the coffee table in my way, knocking over a carafe of ice water and a platter of gold-dusted truffles.

The toilet seat banged open, gaping serene waters like a penny-pool. I lunged forward, hair halving my face as I threw up in warm sour heaves and thick splashes that did not stop but tapered off into weeping.

When I came out, I sat again on the couch, trying to brace myself. How could this have happened?

I pressed my lips together and held myself at the edge of a plush cushion, fingers knotted in my lap. The vent above, set seamlessly into the white-stone wall, heaved almost noiselessly and started to refresh the room with a chilly scented breeze. Where were the windows? This place was a perfect tomb.

Lena opened the door. "Jill's done her very best with him," she announced.

"Jill?" I was aghast. "Why didn't you take him to the hospital?"

"Trust me, she's brilliant. At the hospital he would have been sitting in the waiting room for hours with nothing but aspirin. Besides," she paused, "a hospital would lead to uncomfortable questions." She led me out the door. "No matter; you can take him home now." I followed her up the stairs.

Lena's bob was perfectly smooth, the bangs cutting sharply over her neat brows. And she wore a fresh layer of orange lipstick. I stared at her transfixed, touching my own lips in disbelief. It was insanity that she had gone through the motions, chosen a tube, applied carefully, blotted with a tissue—even as Sawyer lay bleeding in the next room.

Sawyer sat in a side room near the bar, slumped onto a couch underneath his bandages. I raced to him. "Call me this week," Lena said behind me. "Okay? I want to hear updates on him." This, I supposed, was the closest she could come to an apology. "Of course, you'll let me know if there are any complications, right?" I nodded numbly, barely hearing her and unable to take my eyes off Sawyer. "Really," she commanded, and came round in front of me. Putting one finger to my chin, she drew my face toward hers, deliberately. "You'll come to me first. Yes?"

Nodding again, I put a shoulder underneath Sawyer's shoulder and pushed him into a standing position. Still, his head hung down, blocked by bandages, the neck bowed into a near perfect loop with his chest. Lena slipped me the card for a clinic down the street where a client of hers could remove his stitches when it was time, and then put us into a taxi. Before we pulled away, I watched Lena turn smartly on her heels and start tapping into her phone. Was this an ordinary night for her?

On the ride, Sawyer faded in and out from something Jill had given him for the pain. I sat in silence. Once I tried to say something but my voice stuck. Every time I looked at him, where bandage covered half his face, from just below his eye to the jawbone, and then up one arm, I started to cry.

Initially, I had given the driver the address of Sawyer's apartment, but halfway through the ride I realized I would never be able to get him up the stairs, so I had the driver take him to my house instead. I knew Aiden was not there.

"Is that okay?" I asked Sawyer, suddenly doubting myself. "Can I bring you to my place?"

He was leaning heavily on me and didn't seem to hear. When we got to my house, I paid the driver and then helped Sawyer out of the car. The taxi drove off. Nearly his full body weight was upon me as we walked up the path. I fished the keys from my pocket and helped him through the door. Just inside the mud room, we stumbled and fell, though I caught his body at the last moment and heaved him up once more, not sure how I held all his weight. I brought him to my bed and took off his bloody clothes, my motions numb in disbelief when I saw the wounds.

All night, I woke on and off, checking Sawyer's bandages, checking for fever. At one point, he woke too, and when he saw me he recoiled immediately, in animal fear. After a moment, he seemed to remember himself, and relaxed, and then drifted back to sleep. But when I finally got up in the morning, Sawyer was already awake and looking at me a few inches away on the bed. We stared at each other silently, suddenly reduced to being strangers again. It was clear to me that the only reason Sawyer was there was because he had no one else to take care of him.

"Pain pills?" That was all he could mumble.

I scrambled out of bed and found them, fed them to him. Afterward, I also found a new bandage and some athletic tape. He sat on the bed as I took off the old bandage. I sucked in my breath at the lines of stitching.

"Is it bad?" he asked.

"Yes," I said, aghast. "I'm so, so sorry." My voice cracked. "We have to go to the hospital."

"No. I just need to heal now."

"You must be furious," I pushed, stretching out the tape to tear it. "You should be. I don't even know what to say. There are no words for this."

"It was an accident." He spoke decisively, coldly. "Wasn't it?"

I started to speak again, hoping to get him to say the things he had in mind but wouldn't speak. But soon he fell back asleep, so in silence I continued to carefully plaster him back together.

All that day, he moved in and out sleep. Late night he woke again and seemed more alert.

"I'm going downstairs to make tea," I told him.

He started to protest but then just nodded without saying anything. It hurt him to speak. I could see that he was weak. His entire body was hot.

He tried to turn over and then gasped in pain. "You're like my mother. She thinks tea fixes everything." He closed his eyes in a wave of pain. "It doesn't."

By the time the tea had brewed and I carried it upstairs, he was asleep. I sat there holding it for a few minutes, hoping he would wake. But he did not. Eventually, I became restless. Leaving it for him on the nightstand, I went back downstairs to collect my purse and phone. I walked to the store. I put a box of tea in the shopping basket and a tube of antibiotic ointment along with a package of gauze.

After all that had happened, the whole world looked unreal to me. Even this place I knew so well seemed strange. I walked down the street and passed the pub. The manager was erasing the message on the chalkboard outside. Collecting myself, I stopped to watch as *live music* and *two for one tacos* disappeared into gray dust.

When I reached the statue in the square, I stood underneath the 1918 plaque and looked up to its highest point. Why had Jack and I stood so many times below this statue, puzzling about that number, that history? What had made it seem so important? Eventually, I continued walking home, making my way through the neighborhood. All my years here suddenly seemed incomprehensible.

Throughout that night, I remained awake and guarded Sawyer as a mother would. Like my mother, his mother, the mother I always hoped I would be but never was. I would fix him, even if he couldn't be fixed, even if he didn't want to be fixed by me. Had he had anyone else nearby to care for him, I knew he would be gone. But he was alone, so I tended to his bandages, fed him, gave him water and tea when he moaned, and even when he didn't. I watched over him fiercely, changed the soaked clothes and sheets under him, sitting poised at my desk ready to respond to any summons.

The next day, Sawyer and I awoke together. The bleeding had stopped. His scars were starting to heal. For the first time, he was able to take a shower by himself. I heard the sound of the water turning off. There was a wonderful normalcy in the creaking pipes. It gave me hope that somehow through nursing him I had erased some of what happened. But when he got out of the shower, his face was icy.

He came to me, wrapped in a towel. "I was going to stop working with the hijab group."

"You were?" My face lit up. I could hear him again, that night playing guitar at the bar. "Why?"

"For you."

"And for you," I urged him. "Because you want more."

He shook his head. "No." He looked at me plainly now, self-conscious as he spoke, aware of his own resignation and where he was headed. Like an animal in a slaughterhouse that has a brief glimpse of impending doom—its survival instinct sharpens for an instant but then dulls again as it paws realization to the side and follows the herd out to the cool blue pasture. "Maybe I want less."

"You don't mean that."

But his lack of conviction reminded me of an interview I'd read in the newspaper the other day with a man who was a prisoner for years within a terrorist cell. In between praying and torturing him and damning America, his captors had asked him if he could set them up with any western women. Would the men guarding that cell have abandoned their beliefs if they knew it was feasible to have someone warm in bed with them at night, living a Hollywood movie? Would Sawyer's code, too, shift so easily?

The man was still a stranger, really. And yet I felt that same feeling as I did when I went into Aiden's room at night to straighten the covers, moving around the room with a sense of possessiveness. I was moved by him, by what existed between us—which seemed like it was mine, ours. It wasn't his fault. I made him all along into something bigger, some caricature of my own creation and need, forcing importance into everything that happened between us. I tried to gently touch his cheek. It could still be okay.

Sawyer drew away. "I may not know what I want, but I know I don't want this."

And now I saw him as if I had never looked at him closely before. The shadow upon his face; the lurking fear; the faltering mouth that looked too thick-lipped and awkward but so endearing to me. I'd hoped that nursing him back to health would somehow fix us, but now I saw that he was repulsed by me. Redemption had been impossible all along.

18.

One evening, after Christmas and when winter break was almost over, I found myself alone in the kitchen. The place was filled with good smells and such plenty. Potted herbs grew on the windowsills. And there were always so many choices—baskets of cherries and plums and avocados in any season, mangos from far-off lands, warm cookies. The kitchen spilled over with food and yet it was unbearably quiet.

Passing through the silent landscape of small appliances on the countertop—the monolith mixer, the espresso skyscraper, and that big boat of a crockpot anchored at the dock—it occurred to me that all these things were meant to simplify the daily chop and prep and rise of meals, but somehow they just complicated them.

The sight of that crockpot reminded me of those days when Jack and I thought we were pious as we experimented with Kabbalah and tried to observe one holy day of rest each week. For a time, I felt I understood the sense in ritual guidelines, where there was not a free-for-all with food and sex and work, where all the things people seemed to want were already manifest: mindfulness, meditation, being whole with your body.

The people around us in this community were animated and sparkling sometimes, talking about the spirit world, talking Kabbalah, either newly returned or newly enlightened. There were rousing meals and whiskey shots on Shabbat and crowded dinner tables.

But then we went home just ourselves when it was done, Jack and I, to a house where we tried declaring any technology off limits—no lights, no phone, no computer, even no paper and pencil. Nothing operated other than the crockpot, already set on Low, preparing our food for the next day; a peasant's stew of barley, beans, onions, and the fattiest of meats. Those were the quietest days I ever experienced, before or since, when we were unplugged, when the vanishing of hours was marked only by the stew being rendered in the crockpot. The fat and meat fell from the bones and thickened the air with a comforting smell, transforming scents into images and then into slips of stories of animal sacrifices and ancient temples and feasts and pilgrimages, each one drifting into me, feeling real. What a trick, a world at once so real and at the same time imagined—soon slurped up with a spoon, and gone.

In the end, after a few months, Jack and I abandoned the day of rest and eventually the whole Kabbalah thing. We did jigsaw puzzles, then Pilates, then watched old movies instead. Quiet, we had discovered, could be wisps of potential—or merely emptiness.

Trying to shake off that quiet now, I walked from the kitchen that night, through the darkened dining room where Jack and I had sometimes held neighborhood patrol meetings, where we once had holiday meals with his parents and my parents in what had seemed like unbreakable days, lingering over saucy plates and drained wine glasses. And all the while, I had wondered idly, bleakly about some Progressive's Progress. Did anything I do matter?

I left the quiet of my house and wandered back to The Quarter. I went to that old moonshine bar where Sawyer and I once sat. I bought a drink, then two, then six, choking them down till the smooth sugarcane heat softened my misery.

Afterward, waiting in the corridor outside the bar's 'Occupied' bathroom door, I leaned against the wall, growing dizzy and impatient as the minutes ticked by. I closed my eyes to ease my headache. Suddenly the door burst open and Penny Mallow tumbled out. Her dress strap was slipping down one soft arm and her hair was mussed, her skirt cinched up. She held the hand of an older man in a hipster suit, tall with a shock of white blond hair that fell across his face.

"Professor!" Penny gasped, then did a double-take. "You're so drunk!" She giggled in dismay. "What are you doing here?"

"I might ask the same." I drawled. "But I guess I already know." I turned to the man with her. "This, I assume, is Donald."

He looked startled that I knew his name and turned to Penny in a mute question.

"Oh, don't worry." She put a hand on his arm. "She won't say anything."

Donald had thick lusty lips set into a broad face. He wore leather boots, a shiny belt, and a purple snakeskin suit that Penny had probably chosen for him downtown. When he let her dress him up and gave in to the playful, foolish vulnerability of it, of her youth, he trailed behind her, stiff but happy.

Collecting myself, I took a deep breath. For a moment, I felt like I might throw up, but I held it down till the feeling passed. I pictured Penny on the day of her senior project, dancing with stiletto cupcakes, licking the frosting, letting her potential dry up one lap dance at a time. I put my hands at my temples and it seemed that all my wisdom and all my madness were, in the end, exactly the same.

The woody smell of the newly renovated floor planks filled my lungs, also the scents of lavender diffusing from bamboo sticks in the bathroom and the griminess of the plumbing just below. Reading the air as always like a weatherman, I picked up on some possibility in the pregnant, breezeless quiet of that corner, in the fatigue, the after sex letdown that comes when the tiny-death climax fades and the sweat cools and the intensity seems silly and then gives way to a mild existentialism: is this all there is? Logic might be clear and inverted in that space in time; perhaps she'd listen and really hear.

My hand gripped her arm, the soft inside of it, and suddenly we were face to face, so close I could have kissed her. I smelled Chapstick and moonshine on her mouth.

"You have every opportunity," I began. But what could I really know about her life? I grasped at the straws, remembering Ruth's article. "There are millions of others around the world, child brides, child soldiers. They don't have even a fraction of the choices you have."

Penny flipped her hair. "Child bride? That would never be me. I would just walk away. Nothing could stop me."

"Where would you go?" I muttered.

Penny shrugged as if such questions didn't merit an answer. "I choose. All of it."

I understood, maybe for the first time, what I had seen of myself in her. Didn't all people just want the power to define themselves?

"You can choose what you like, sure. But you have all the privilege in the world. And if you choose *this*, then you don't have half the imagination you tell yourself you have."

For once, the girl who always had an answer for everything was left gape-mouthed, moved not by what I had said but by my own misery seeping through it. She was disturbed to finally see some of herself in me. And when she looked at Donald, middle-aged and drying-out too, she grew disgusted by him, also, that she had let him latch on to her.

At the entrance to The Quarter, Penny turned away from him and walked off, leaving him behind. Donald stood, looking in her direction with disbelief, even hurt. But when she didn't glance back, he sneered and straightened and moved off with long strides into another part of The Quarter.

For a while he did not pay attention to where he was going. But eventually Donald found himself by the Colosseum. Stopping short in an archway, he surveyed the humanity under the shadows of faux-ancient columns. Then, across the way, he spotted a woman who seemed to be looking out over everything too and waiting— waiting for him. Anji. She saw him, a tall blond mountain in a snakeskin suit. And when he summoned her, that was the sign.

She brought this half-man, half-snake back to her room at the old plant, her fingers lightly touching the suede scales of his suit as they walked. And after the thing was done, as he passed out for a moment, she pulled the cloudy sheet around her and went down the hall then down the stairs to the large factory-like room below. The old cook stove in the corner was spewing dungy smoke. Anji went straight to the large containers of ghee and kerosene stored nearby, and gently, gently tipped them one by one in the direction of the fire, walking calmly back out to the hall even as the liquids poured steadily forward, advancing towards the stove until they ignited.

"Fire!" one of the older women screamed. Then all those youth creams and beauty lotions and fatty oils and paints nearby now quickly caught fire too, and the one cracked smoke detector that actually had some batteries went off. On every floor, they heard the alarm, and young girls in braids poured from the rooms out into the crowd in the narrow hallway. Old men in the hallways on the top floor, half-dressed, grabbed their wallets and stumbled out, still stiff. They padded around with their boxers and wide white calves, irritated as if it was all just a drill. After all, every empire has thought that exactly where it stands is where human history has always been leading to. No one really thought the stragglers over the borders or the cracks in their leaders or small stirrings of revolution—or a fire alarm down the hall—signaled an existential reckoning. And even after it was clear, the fire was real, the men tried to give orders, this way and that, as if by their direction the fire could be controlled and talked into extinguishing itself.

The concoction of chemicals at the center of the fire now exhaled with a supernatural heat, smoking and spiraling, transforming what would have been an ordinary building fire into a fierce inferno. The smoke became thick. People coughed and shouted in panic and covered their mouths. Once the fire crept up the stairs, it was clear there was no way they would ever leave through the front door. People raced back into the rooms to look for window exits. Some rooms had no windows at all, or they opened onto a brick wall. Some of the windows were barred and people there spent their last moments of life trying to conjure up superhuman powers to somehow bend the metal. That's where they found them in coming days, charred.

One girl discovered salvation in her room: her window had a fire escape. "Here," she called to others in the hallway. Even in rooms without a fire escape, they crashed chairs through the glass and people jumped out, breaking their bones in relief. For others caught in the hallway, it was too late.

I had thought that maybe I could save Anji someday, but in the end she saved us, this ninety-pound prostitute who never made it out of the building herself.

Outside, people watched the fire and expected the firemen to put it out and to impose order again. Seated on the curb, they tweeted and snapped selfies to record the moment. But this blaze turned out to be an otherworldly fire, inextinguishable.

Soon, the flames turned fierce again. "Back!" the police yelled to the crowd of spectators. "Get back! Get out of here!" The crowd rose from the curb and began to run uptown.

From the black distance of stars and space and time, it is hard to pin down a singular event that changes a planet—there's rarely one apocalyptic day like in the old movies, when a virus is unleashed or zombies rise or aliens invade. Real breakdowns are more gradual, after all. The world has changed since those days of plenty before the fire, perhaps for hundreds of reasons. Maybe from the crash in the markets that followed, or the spate of hurricanes and floods a few weeks later which devastated some part of every continent. Certainly, the years of trembling reconstruction that followed were pocked with bouts of aggression between people and governments that altered our very fiber. But to my worn eyes, it was the fire itself that defined both the moment and the aftermath.

The smoke and flames tore into the night sky again and then started to consume The Quarter around it. Fire swallowed whole buildings, stores and cafes and the straw tiki bar where beautiful Penny probably sat. Fire poured into all the nests of men studying holy texts and into the underground tunnels, even into the Prongs labyrinth, where I imagined Lena and Philip were probably toasting each other in the hall of slaves, cackling and carefree until the very end. Fire snaked even to the streets of the wider district where Aiden would have been walking with some of his friends. It quickly closed out seemingly separate roads and sectors and paths trapping the whole place in a singular ocean of smoke and flames, greedily eating all inside, even, God help me, my Aiden.

Days of smoke. Chaos. Searching, searching among the missing thousands. Then the unavoidable truth. Among the many dead, my own child.

A child lost means there is never whole pleasure or peaceful sleep again. It is replaced by a nightmare of his final moments that perpetually rewinds. I'd spent so many years hunting for some wise man, or a man that would love me, when all along the only man that mattered was the one growing up under my own roof—every mundane moment with him, because all the moments would be so few. Trying to memorialize that being—that magical, fleeting fusion of flesh and soul—seems so empty, as if a name carved into some stone, as if anything at all, could bring even the smallest sense of relief.

In the days after the fire, the stores that still stood across the city went empty. Garbage lined the ashy streets un-serviced. All that rotting trash was an affront and a shock at the beginning. Suddenly, outrageously, money and influence meant little. It was the cockroaches who feasted freely, scuttling around us in a swarm, like plump mejool dates, having bided their time for millennia. It made everyone panic. But I just watched the cockroaches numbly, wishing only to die also, to be consumed by the insects myself.

Soon after, the storms struck. There had been storms before, and we had always worried that the rising, warming seas could be coming for us, one lick at a time. But now they left behind cruel, immediate layers of devastation and an undeniable reality.

All that had once been was gone for good. So people started to rise into a new normalcy, using skills and instinct they never knew they had, picking the trash clean and tinkering with broken things. And eventually, still dazed, with every movement of my bones heavy and slow but bent on survival, I joined them.

One day, my trash picking led me through what was left of The Quarter. I came to the area that had housed Robby's place of study, where I once fleetingly thought to sit with him and the people who studied under him, to read ancient texts and eat brown rice and pretend I believed in magic. The building was gone, of course, the beams and books and stained glass all indistinguishable rubble.

Robby and most of the other men had been killed in the fire, but there, in the flat expanse that was meant to be their backyard garden, I saw a few of his disciples who had survived, digging through the ash and soil. Their faces looked more placid than other survivors; perhaps their simple bread and learning braced them better for this era. But still they knew little.

"Will anything grow?" I asked.

One man leaned on his tool. "Maybe soon." He pointed at some green shoots.

I crouched with them in the dirt to study the concoction of soil and cinders glutted by floodwater. Putting out a palm, I took up a handful of the mud, like I remembered seeing my grandmother do, and a red earthworm raised itself from the clay and ruin.

"Worms are good," the man said.

I nodded, let the dirt fall back to the ground, and went to look for a tool. There, by a collection of buckets, I saw a hammer, an old broom handle with a slice of metal affixed by twine, a rusty rake. I took the rake. Gripping its corroded handle, I chose a corner of the field. The man came to show me how to turn the soil, pulling the rake line after line in long muscled stretches. "You bring up the good dirt from deep below, see, and mix it with the garbage at the surface. Soon, maybe, it could be all healthy again." As he left, I continued raising the good earth with a peasant's hunch and sweat, morphing little by little into some other kind of creature.

The man came again later with some water for me to drink. He had that clear-eyed look that I remember people had on my grandmother's farm, when toil and tasks provided purpose. He looked around at my work and nodded approvingly. "You've made progress."

I nodded and held up my hands to show him the blisters, already raw. Eventually, they would harden into callouses, like paws. Yet they would have to do. Stripped of conveniences and much of the old knowledge, we were all so very, very clumsy at survival. But for the sake of the ashes, we tried to be worthy of this last blessed chance.

Acknowledgements

Thank you to David Ross and Kelly Huddleston for all their work in birthing this book. To Michelle Montifar, Yuberkys Fryer, Judith Birnbaum, Cynthia Kane, Michael Neff, and all the other villagers, jumpstarts, and muses along the way. Thank you to my parents for the example of their love, and to my siblings, the tightest squad that ever was. Finally, endless gratitude to my husband—adventurer and counterpoint—and to the three shining souls at our table.